GUIRGUIS THE TORCHBEARER

By
IRIS HABIB EL-MASRY

ST MARY & MOSES ABBEY PRESS

Guirguis the Torchbearer
By Iris Habib El-Masry
Edited and Illustrated by Sara Iskandar

Designed & Published by:
St. Mary & St. Moses Abbey Press
101 S Vista Dr, Sandia, TX 78383
stmabbeypress.com

Library of Congress Control Number: 2022941346

To the beloved departed who, though unseen by our physical eys, are nonetheless linked to us by the strongest of all invisible powers, the power of love. Accordingly, they have helped us by their prayer and by their influence, thus sustaining us in our life as we strive along day by day.

Contents

Foreword

"And others were tortured, not accepting deliverance; that they might obtain a better resurrection" (Heb. 11:35).

By these words, St. Paul described our holy fathers, the brave martyrs, who had many chances to avoid suffering and martyrdom, but instead refused because they were looking for a better resurrec-tion. They knew that the cross is the essence of their discipleship to the Lord. So they carried the cross happily, and they rejoiced in their pains. They preferred to suffer affliction with the people of God than to enjoy the pleasures of sin for a season.

The Coptic Church, the mother of the martyrs, during her history, suffered many afflictions and persecutions that added more brightness to her glory and more depth to her spirituality. Though she is still struggling against unseen powers of the darkness, yet she is indeed a victorious Church through the grace of her Beloved Groom.

This excellent novel, by the well-known historian Iris Habib El-Masry, draws a picture of the Copts' history in the first half of the eight century. We offer many thanks to the souls of our beloved and faithful writer, who used her pen during all her life with all cleverness, to record the church history from the first century until the middle of the twentieth century. We ask the Lord to repose her soul in the Paradise of Joy and to reward her for all of her services to the Church with the heavenly reward. We also ask her to pray on our behalf before the throne of God that we may continue to bear the torch and hand it to our followers as we received it from our holy ancestors. I'd like also to thank all those who contributed to this book, including and especially the departed Ms. Dora Habib El-Masry for bringing this valuable novel to light. We ask our Lord to use it for the edification of its readers.

We ask our Lord, God and Savior Jesus Christ, the true light of the world, to enlighten our hearts and souls that we may conduct our lives in a way that is pleasing to Him and be faithful wit-nesses for Him. We ask this through the intercession of the Most Holy Virgin, the Mother of God St. Mary, St. Mark the Evangelist, and all the venerable martyrs.

Bishop Youssef
Bishop of the Coptic Orthodox Diocese
of the Southern United States

Preface by the Editor

On What It Means to Be a Torchbearer

A few years ago, as I was preparing for my church's annual book fair, I stumbled across an old copy of "Guirguis the Torchbearer." I had never seen this book before. What was even more striking was that the author of this book was none other than the great Coptic historian, Iris Habib El-Masry, the renowned author of the monumental *Story of the Copts*. This particular little book I had found, however, seemed fictional in nature, and nobody seemed to know it existed.

I took the book home with me, eager to know its contents. Perhaps initially, I was expecting to get nothing out of it but a good read during my moments of leisure. I quickly realized that between my hands was a gem—a valuable stone of great price that had been buried in a box of old, torn magazines for nearly two decades.

I read and became acquainted with Guirguis, the protagonist of this novel, who was commanded by his brother to be a "torchbearer" in the community he lived in, thus fulfilling Christ's commandment to be a "light unto the world." The setting of this novel, as well as the historical circumstances, are based on real facts. Guirguis lived in eighth-century Egypt, during the reign of the ruthless Muslim Caliph, Marwan II of Umayyad (reigned from 744–750). Although very little is known and said about eighth-century Egypt, especially about the Copts who lived during that dark time, El-Masry brilliantly portrays all of the monumental scenes and brings to life names that would have long been forgotten in history.

During the days of Caliph Marwan, Christians suffered severe persecution. Taxes were raised on the Christians, who were considered "dhimmis" or "protected persons" in Islamic society. As such, they were required to pay the "jizya," or taxes reserved for non-believers, and had certain restrictions, but were otherwise equal in terms of property and obligations (this equality, historically, has been more theoretical than practical). Moreover, Christians were pressured to either convert to Islam, or suffer intolerable persecutions, many times leading to death. In response to the increasing jizya and the oppression, riots broke out in 748. The leader of the Coptic faction in Upper Egypt was none other than John of Samanoud (known in this novel by his Coptic name, Youannis). Marwan, believing that the rebellion was due to incitement by the Coptic Patriarch, had him imprisoned and tortured. The name of this great Patriarch, who endured such suffering, is not mentioned in this novel; my own research has determined him to be Pope Khail I (Also known as "Michael" or "Mikhail," whose feast day is Bashans 12. See Appendix A).1

---

1   Robert Morgan, *History of the Coptic Orthodox People and the Church of Egypt* (Victoria, Canada: Friesen Press, 2006), 296–303.

El-Masry, being the scholar she was, traveled the world over to gain knowledge on her beloved Coptic Church. While in La Bibliotheque Nationale in Paris, she stumbled across an Arabic manuscript that described the reign of Marwan, and of a believer in his court who swayed him to take gentler measures with the Coptic Prelate (see the author's foreword). El-Masry wrote about it in her *magnum opus*, *The Story of the Copts*:

> During that period of hardship and travail, God's Mercy overshadowed His people in the appointment of a devoted Copt as superintendent over the governor's table. Succeeding in winning great favor with the governor, he was able to get permission to visit Abba Mikhail and his companions in their prison daily, and carried to them whatever they needed of food and clothes."[2]

Thus, the fictional character of Guirguis was born in the imagination of this great writer. His unwavering faith in God and wittiness serve as an example to us of how we ought to behave in the face of adversity. Taking the metaphorical "torch" from first his brother, then from the gentle Bishop Moussa of Wissim, he bore the light first entrusted to us by Christ Himself (Matt. 5:14). The result of his bravery and piety is the love he won from the Muslim *wali* (or governor), and ultimately, the peace that resulted in Egypt after many travails. Thus, in his young age, Guirguis did by God's grace what was seemingly impossible and became an example of

---

2   Iris Habib El-Masry, *The Story of the Copts* (Newberry Springs, CA: St. Anthony Monastery, 1982), 50.

the words of Bishop Moussa, "Our lives are in our Father's hands—whether they are to be short or long does not count. What counts is the use we make of them."

Bishop Moussa of Wissim, Pope Mikhail, and John of Samanoud are not names that are often mentioned in the Coptic community; I daresay, only those who have studied in some sort of seminary would even recognize them. Their legacy is overshadowed by the darkness of the age they lived in and by the names of the other "giants" of the Coptic Church (a few of which are mentioned in this very novel. Many lived during the fourth century, a period of great prosperity in church history). Nonetheless, we cannot even fathom what our Church would be like today if they had not been brave enough to withstand the pressures of their time, and to bear the torches of their faith through political storms. We owe it to El-Masry for doing the hard work in researching these Dark Ages, and spoon-feeding us with this history in the form of an entertaining and edifying novel.

Here, one ought to take a moment to further speak about Iris Habib El-Masry. Many are aware of her literary achievements. On a personal level, I respect her more so for being a lady pioneer during a time when many people in the society she lived in did not pursue such ambitious intellectual undertakings. In today's age, and in the Western world in particular, the role of women in society is often discussed, disputed, and confused.[3] Thankfully, our church is rich with examples of heroines who were strong leaders in their

---

3 Ironically, the writing of this introduction was the same day as the second annual "Woman's March" in Washington D.C., where thousands took to the streets demanding gender equality, amongst other political issues—including abortion. Sadly, abortion has now become a "women's rights" issue, thus detracting the naive from the main core of this grave sin, which is murder of a live fetus.

own rights, such as the lady martyrs St. Marina, St. Barbara, St. Agatha, and St. Rifkah. These are just a few examples of the women "torchbearers" who were victorious in their sufferings, despite the fact that it was their womanhood that made them seemingly vulnerable.[4] In the modern age, there are two famous examples that demonstrate what it means to be a woman in the Coptic Church. The first one is the beloved Tamav Erene.[5] The second is the author of this book, the great scholar Iris Habib El-Masry.

El-Masry was born to an affluent Coptic family in 1910. Her father, Habib Pasha El-Masry (1885–1953), was the General Secretary of the *Majlis El-Shura*, or the Consultative Council of the upper house of the Egyptian Parliament.[6] She had two brothers and three sisters, each one pursuing a unique career and leading an active role in their community. She received a Bachelor in Arts, and went on to specialize in education at the University of London in 1932. Having loved the life of learning, she went back to school to do research in Dropsie College[7] in 1955. During her life, she authored dozens of books, her most famous being *The*

---

4   St. Marina was wooed by a pagan official (who found her beautiful) to forsake her faith and marry him, and she was tortured and martyred for refusing. St. Barbara was betrayed by her own father when he found out she became Christian. St. Agatha, as one of her tortures, had her breasts cut off. St. Rifkah (or Rebecca) watched all of her children slaughtered before her very eyes for the sake of their faith.

5   Tamav Erene (1936-2006) was an outstanding figure in modern Coptic history. She became Mother Superior of the convent of Abu Seifan in Old Cairo, despite being the youngest nun in her convent at the time. She is famous for her leadership in renovating, renewing, and expanding the convent. She also performed many miracles during her life, and even after her passing. Although she was ailed with illness for many years, yet she continued her service with rigor, faithfulness, and love. Her life touched the hearts of millions around the world.

6   This Council was dissolved in 2013, and abolished by the 2014 Constitution. The Egyptian Parliament has since been a unicameral legislature.

7   Now known as the Katz Center at the University of Pennsylvania.

Story of the Copts. Her other notable books include writings on the role of women in the Coptic Church, a topic she was passionate about. Being the spiritual daughter of the saintly father Abouna Pishoy Kamel,[8] she also wrote his biography. Sadly, these writings have been left untranslated, though there is great need for them in the Western world.

For more on El-Masry's academic achievements, see *A Portrait of a Historian*, Appendix B.

Although El-Masry is famous for her literary and scholarly achievements, many of us may not be aware that she was also a politician. Following in her father's footsteps, she was appointed to the Consultative Council of the Egyptian Parliament in 1980 by President Anwar Sadat. This was a tumultuous time for the Coptic Church, as there were great strains between the Church and the government, as well as persecution of Christians at the hands of Islamic extremists. At one point, El-Masry was brave enough to reason with President Sadat to make a good gesture to the Coptic Church. It is said that Sadat answered her positively, even admitting that he read *The Story of the Copts* which she wrote and expressing his wishes for the Church to regain its glorious status.[9] It is fascinating to think that El-Masry seemed to have taken on a similar role to that of her protagonist Guirguis: just as he used his political power and good relations with the *wali* to help his people, El-Masry did the very same. Even the progression of history between the two eras is ironically similar: both leaders would eventually

---

8   Father Pishoy Kamel (1931-1979) was a saintly Coptic priest known for his active service in the Church. He founded many parishes in Egypt and America. He departed on March 21, 1979 after succumbing to cancer.

9   "Iris Habib el-Masry: A Pioneer of Coptic Feminine Theology," *Coptic Church Review*, Volume 30.2 (Fall/Winter 2009): 52.

put the Coptic Pope under arrest, and their lives were even met with similar fates.[10]

To talk about El-Masry's fascinating life would require an entire book dedicated to her. Her sister, Dora Habib El-Masry, continued her legacy by writing extensively on her. Furthermore, this very book was published posthumously by Dora El-Masry, who found it as a manuscript within her sister's files. Whether or not this manuscript was "complete" as Iris El-Masry had intended it will remain unknown to us forever, but what is certain is that she was passionate about the history of her beloved Church, and she wished to pass the torch of our forefathers unto her readers.

What, then, does it mean to be a "torchbearer?" Are we to read about it in this book passively, being that they are merely words in a fictional work of literature? Or is there an important message that the author is trying to relay to us?

Not only do each of us have the potential of being a torchbearer, but we are actually commanded to bear that torch so that all can see our light—that is, the light of Christ. It is true that we ought to do so by bearing virtues and the fruits of the spirit (Gal. 5:22), but with that is also the necessity to use our talents. Each and every one of us has been given a talent that we are not only supposed to use, but also to invest in (see Matt. 25:14–30). Some can sing and teach hymns beautifully, others can recapture the beauty of God's creation in a painting, others can write poetry. But some of us may have some "nontraditional" gifts. The author of this book is one of the Coptic Church's biggest

---

10 President Sadat would eventually put the Coptic Pope at the time, Pope Shenouda III, under house arrest in September 1981. He was assassinated a little over a month later after doing so.

history buffs; she could have used it to complete all sorts of crossword puzzles and trivia games. Instead, she invested it to glorify God and His saints, and just one fruit of her expansive garden is within your very hands at this moment. No talent is better than the other in God's eyes; He has given to each according to His wisdom, and He only cares that you offer what you were given with a cheerful heart.

Before concluding, I would like to extend my utmost gratitude to those who have supported me and helped me during this project, and most especially to St. Moses Abbey Press for being willing to reintroduce this lovely text. May God bless you all with His bounty, and keep the flame of your torches burning for many years, in joy and prosperity.

And with that, I would like to conclude by saying the following: Iris Habib El-Masry was a torchbearer in her own right. What a shame it would be if time and our own ignorance put out her fire.

May God be glorified forevermore.

Sara Iskandar
Tubah 13, 1734
January 21, 2018
The Feast of the Wedding of Cana of Galilee
The Martyrdom of Lady Demiana and the 40 Virgins

Introduction by the Author

Dear Readers:

In order that you may really enjoy this novel, it is necessary for you to form a clear picture of its historical background.

In the year 61 A.D., St. Mark the Evangelist and Apostle came to Alexandria where he sowed the Seed and received the martyr's crown in 68 AD. Short though his stay was, it was enough for founding the church now knowns as the the Coptic Church (i.e., the Egyptian Church). From 68–194 A.D., this church enjoyed real peace. Commenting on this heavenly state, the Reverend John Neale said:

> It pleased God that the Church which was afterwards to be exposed to such fierce persecutions, and to struggle for its very existence with heresy under two forms,[11] should in its infancy be in great measure protected from the storms which fell upon it from its sister churches. The true faith took deep root, and in due season gave forth fruit to perfection. During the

---

11 Namely, Arianism and Nestorianism.

first two centuries, Egypt enjoyed unusual quiet.[12]

From 194–641 A.D., twenty-one persecutions raged agains the Church, first from Pagan Rome, then from Christian Constantinople. These persecutions were, however, declared by imperial edicts; trials, though mock, were enacted. The toll of blood paid by the Egyptians for their faith was so great that Tertiellian, a priest from Carthage from the latter second century said, "If the martyrs throughout the world were to be put on one side of a scale, and the Coptic martyrs on the other, the latter would outweigh the former." Mr. Guerin, in La Dictinnaire des Dictionnaires, under the heading of "martyr," said that the Copts killed by Emperor Diocletian from 293–303 A.D. numbered 800,000.

From the middle of the seventh century until the end of the eighteenth, no persecution was formally declared, and no royal edict heralded it. Peace or strife rested in the hands of the ruler: if he were kind, the people enjoyed peace under his sway; if cruel, they suffered under his yoke. During these twelve centuries, personal ties were of great importance— they made or marred the general tone of politics. Time and agin, the friendship or enmity of one man was enough to stem the tide or to swam the land in blood.

Marwan II reigned from 744–750 A.D. His was a reign of terror throughout the East. During this era shaken by war and revolt, and Arabic manuscript kept in La Bibliotheque Nationale in Paris described as a historical fragment says

---

12 *History of the Holy Eastern Church*, Volume 1, Page 12.

that there was a believer who sat the King's table, and spoke well of the Patriarch and his fiends who, at that time, were imprisoned. This unknown believer so swayed the king that he ordered the release of the Prelates.

This short statement set my imagination at work. The unknown believer is Guirguis, the hero of this novel. Abba Moussa, the bishop of Wissim, and Youannis of Samanoud are real figures; Youannis was the general of the army in a revolt which actually took place.

With the fall of Marwan II, the Abbasid began their reign, the greatest among them being Haroun El-Rashid of legendary fame. They inaugurated an era of peace.

Thus, this novel is historical in its essentials; the vicissitudes and the good fortune of its hero, though fictitious, could be true, as they describe how the the Wali exercised absolute power.

Therefore dear reader, I hope this novel will give you a picture of that history of Egypt which is unknown to tourists, as well as to the foreigner in general, and will be exciting enough to incite you towards more knowledge of those people who endeavored to bear the Torch aloft from age to age.

I.H. El-Masry

CHAPTER ONE

The Beginning

The first rays of the sun shot across the horizon when Mariam woke up. She tiptoed noiselessly to the eastern corner of her room and offered her morning prayers before the icon of the Virgin Mary.

She was presently joined by her husband, who was famously known as 'Big Brother.' When both of them ended their prayers, Mariam went about her household duties while Big Brother got ready to go downstairs.

At breakfast, Big Brother was a little pensive, and Mariam watched him in silence. Presently, he got up to leave and as he bade his wife goodbye, he said as usual, "Do remember me in your prayers this morning."

Mariam held his hand in both hers and looked straight into his eyes, as he looked back into hers with his warm gentleness and said, "The Lord keep watch over you and I while we are absent from one another." Warmly pressing her

St. Mary, the Mother of God

two hands within his, Big Brother went out.

The day was one of those exceedingly hot days of June. Mariam had all the housework finished early and closed all the shutters to keep the house cool. She repeated the Terce and Sext[13] prayers at their appointed hours, and lingered a little longer in thought over her husband's pensiveness.

At lunch time, Guirguis walked in from school. Before sitting at the table, he asked, "Will Big Brother come for lunch?"

Mariam looked astonished and answered, "You know he never comes for lunch. Why are you asking?"

Guirguis answered, "I was a little late in waking up and only waved him goodbye from my window, so I was half-hoping to find him as I came in."

Mariam was puzzled. She had some misgivings since the morning, and now Guirguis added to these misgivings by his questions.

She was silent for a while, then tried to dispel her own restlessness by asking Guirguis about school. When lunch was over, each retired for the midday rest—but neither of them slept. Mariam repeated the Nones, and for a long while kept kneeling before the icon of St. Mary.

Her meditations were abruptly broken by a quick instant knock on her door. Shenouti rushed in to say, "My lady—pardon me—but Big Brother is on his way here and will you..."

---

13 The prayers mentioned are the third and sixth hours of the Agpeya, or the Coptic book of hours. They correspond to 9 A.M. and noon, respectively. There are a total of seven prayer hours in the Agpeya, from Prime (the morning prayer) to the Midnight prayers. Each hour corresponds to an event in the Life of Christ.

Mariam looked at the boy closely, quite alarmed. "What is it?" she asked.

Shenouti took a deep breath, then said in a voice that was barely above a whisper, "Will you prepare for him his bed? He wants to have a rest."

"What is it?" Mariam again reiterated.

Shenouti was silent for a while, walked up to the icon of the blessed Virgin murmuring, "Help me, my Lady," crossed himself, then came back to Mariam and said, "I will tell you the whole truth. The Prince was very ill-tempered today— the heat, some letters he received from the Caliph, I don't know what. Anyhow, he was sour. Some of his courtiers were trying to amuse him, and one of them laughingly suggested that he should try some new sport to banish his care. He maliciously said, 'Here is your hand dagger, don't you think it would be fun to play target?' At which the Prince said, 'Oh yes, let's have a hand at it.' He started throwing his dagger at different things in his room and presently—"

Mariam cut in, "Don't complete the story. I know. Where is Big Brother wounded?"

"In the breast."

"Very sorely wounded?"

"Well, the court doctor said it is not serious, but who knows?"

Mariam hastily prepared the bed, then asked, "Did Guirguis hear?"

"Well strange enough, Master Guirguis was at the gate of our quarter as I came in."

"At the gate! On such a hot day!"

"Yes, my lady."

"He did look restless at lunch."

The sound of footsteps cut in on the conversation, and they both went out to the door. Big Brother was seated on a chaise carried by two guards and followed by Guirguis, Dr. Pakhom, and a few others. Mariam led the way to the bedroom, and when Big Brother was put on it, the doctor ordered everyone out except Mariam. Even Guirguis was refused admittance. Dr. Pakhom made a thorough study of his patient, gently dressed his wound, then gave him some medicine. A few minutes later, Big Brother was asleep.

The doctor and Mariam went to a corner and sat down on a low divan. He said, "The wound is not too big, but it is deep and it is evident that it was thrust with force. It is also evident that Big Brother bled a lot. You know that our lives are in the hands of the Father. You also know how much I (and everybody else) love Big Brother. I will endeavor to do my best for him. You pray for him, and... I know that you have always been able to keep a calm demeanor."

Mariam answered quite calmly, though her voice was almost a whisper, "Thank you very much doctor. I know your love and your sincerity. But what about Guirguis?"

"Leave him to me."

The doctor gave her a few orders in case Big Brother should wake before his return, then took his leave.

Outside, Guirguis was pacing back and forth like a caged lion, looking very pale, and asking broken questions every now and then to Shenouti, who was close at his heels. When the doctor appeared, Guirguis ran towards him and scanned his face imploringly.

The doctor said "Guirguis, my dear lad, be steady. Big Brother is now sleeping peacefully and all he needs is a good rest."

"But is it serious, Doctor?"

"Somewhat serious, but we must all do what we can to help him recover."

"What can I do?"

"Be as calm as you can and remember him in your prayers."

"Prayers? That is what I have been doing ever since I could utter a word. Big Brother is a father, mother, and brother to me. I shall pray as I never prayed before."

"And don't forget to be calm."

"I'll try."

The doctor left at these words.

***

It was the third day since Big Brother was stabbed. Everybody in the Coptic quarter walked quietly and spoke in whispers, as though they were in the room of the wounded man. Even the little children forgot their play and were solemn. For Big Brother was thus called by everyone there. He was the richest and most influential man among them, and he lived in accordance with the injunctions of Christ: regarding everyone as a brother, giving of his time and money to all, and always exerting his influence in the court to ward off any wrong or injustice. And now—here he lay.

Even Dr. Pakhom had no word of comfort to give to those who asked; this big-hearted Christian lay dying because of the whim of a malicious courtier and an irresponsible ruler. But will God not vindicate His people, when He is the One Who said, "Vengeance is mine?"[14]

And yet, "How long, Oh Lord, how long?"[15]

In the room, the dying man asked for his young brother Guirguis. The lad came in and knelt beside the bed, laying his hand on his brother's. His eyes were blazing, adding to the pallor of his face.

Big Brother spoke in slow, measured tones conveying hope and confidence. He said, "Guirguis, my brother, our lives are in the hands of our Father, and our Holy Church teaches us that whether we are in the body or out of the body, we are always linked together. Those here pray for the departed, and the departed pray for those here. Hence, prayer is the spiritual invisible chain that binds our spirits. Those who have gone on before us have given the glorious example of being faithful unto the end, and we must follow in their footsteps. When one torchbearer falls, those behind must pick the torch up and keep the flame ablaze, for ours must be the Light that never fails. You are still young, but you have attained the age at which our Blessed Savior went into the Temple.[16] To you do I entrust the Torch, and my prayers will always be with you to uphold you. I know that by God's Grace you shall be worthy of the name you bear, and worthy of the great heritage bequeathed to us by those who lived and died for Christ. And now, bend down and kiss

---

14 Deut. 32:35

15 Psalm 13:1.

16 That is, twelve years old (Luke 2:41-52).

me. God speed until that day when we shall meet yonder."

The young lad did as he was told, and Big Brother added, "And now kindly call in Mariam."

***

By sunset, the last flow of life had ebbed out of Big Brother, and he was lying with a smile on his benign face. The candles were lit around him, and the Blessed Virgin's eyes seemed full of tenderness as she looked down on him from the icon.

Dr. Pakhom had succeeded in sending even Mariam and Guirguis away, and the only person keeping vigil was an old monk who had known Big Brother ever since he was a toddler.

A few hours after midnight, the old monk was dozing when Guirguis tiptoed into the room and knelt by the side of his brother's bed. He looked into the face he adored and once more heard the words spoken to him a few hours earlier. He did not know how long he knelt there—it did not matter how long—all that Big Brother did and said passed before him, and he relived his experiences as far back as he could remember up to the last moment. Then he gently put his hand over the bandage that hid the fatal wound and swore that he would get revenge. At that very moment, the old monk became fully awake and conscious of his presence. He gently knelt beside him and together, the two recited the prayers of Dawn.

***

Weeks passed—but Guirguis was still pale. His eyes sunk deeper and deeper, blazing out more fierily. He ate very little and slept little. He seemed unconscious of everything and everybody. He had not shed a single tear ever since he had seen his brother coming back stabbed. Mariam prayed that God in His mercy would make him cry—if only he could cry—so that perhaps his burden will lift a little. None dared to speak to him. Shenouti was the only one who kept him company wherever he went—Shenouti, who had to tell the story of the fatal wound over and over again to his young master, and who was his only comforter.

Then in September, when the Copts celebrated their New Year,[17] Abba Moussa, bishop of Wissim,[18] came to visit the family. He stayed with them for a few weeks. He was a venerable old man. His face was wrinkled with age, and he had a flowing white beard, but his eyes twinkled and shone like those of a young man. Anyone looking into those eyes felt the joy of life. No one could believe that such youthful and joyful eyes were really those of a wrinkled old man.

The bishop had come in answer to Mariam's plea, and

---

17 The Coptic New Year falls on Thoth (Tute) 1, or September 11 of the Gregorian calendar. The Coptic calendar is based on the ancient Egyptian calendar. The first of Thoth corresponds with the inundation of the Nile, which covered the land of Egypt. Thus, the Coptic calendar is also a highly agricultural one.

18 Wissim was an ancient city in the Nile Delta, located about 25 kilometers south of Cairo. It was a great bishopric until the 14th century(it is said that the largest cathedral in Egypt at that time was located there), but now it is part of the Giza bishopric. Several of its bishops were martyred. Abba Moussa (or Bishop Moses in English), was a true figure in history. He was an outstanding confessor, and despite the numerous persecutions he endured, he lived almost a century. It was he who nominated Pope Mikhail I to the papal throne.

Guirguis who had always admired and revered the bishop responded to him with amazing rapidity. For the bishop had drunk life's cup to its dregs; he had known its sorrows and its joys, he had listened to the endless tales of humanity and seen how noble and how ignoble Man could be. His love for his people was as boundless as was his faith in God. And this love, together with the joy he radiated over all who came near him, made everyone ready to come to him and listen to whatever he had to say. Guirguis was certainly attracted to him—a little diffidently at first—but soon he sought after him eagerly. For the old man never preached nor reproached—he only told stories that elated and inspired him.

So within a week's time, he unburdened his soul to the old man and received from him words of comfort and hope and regained his confidence in life. Gradually, Guirguis became the lad he was. A month later, as Abba Moussa was bidding him goodbye, he made him promise to live up to Big Brother's expectations and to carry on his duties as a man. He also invited him to come to Wissim as soon as the school year was over.

***

Early in June, Guirguis set off for Wissim and took Shenouti with him. Together, they embarked on one of the white-masted ships which floated over the Nile since time immemorial. They started at dawn and watched the first rays of the sun as they shot through the eastern sky. Guirguis stood entranced; he had seen the sun rise many a time, for whenever he traveled with Big Brother, they had always set out early. But today, the river and the fields seemed to be bathed in glory, and the whole scene filled him with a sense of awe and peace. As he watched the light growing and bursting forth into the "great sun," his memory unfurled before him all of the year's events. It was only yesterday that they celebrated the Liturgy in commemoration of Big Brother. Yes, it was a year ago that this most fateful event happened. How strange it is that he should feel peace filling his soul while thinking of Big Brother in spite of his great sorrow. But had not Big Brother told him that he will be praying for him? That peace which so invaded him now was surely the fruit of those prayers.

The ship glided over the waters very smoothly, for Father Nile was still asleep. Gradually as they moved, life began to stir on either shore, and soon there was movement and shouting as other ships crossed their way and as the cattle and the *fellaheen*[19] began their daily tasks. The boatman hummed their nostalgic tunes which echoed and reechoed on the river across the generations. The fellaheen droned out their songs to the rhythm of the *sakeya*, or the water wheel. All these were familiar to Guirguis and Shenouti, who stood side-by-side at the end of the ship, observing everything around them as though it was a new world. They were both eagerly looking ahead for the great bishopric of Wissim and its marvels. More so, it was the old bishop who could still see life with the eyes of youth whom they were eagerly seeking.

Three hours later, the ship lay anchor. On the quay, two men with four donkeys stood waiting for them, and with them came a porter with a little cart. One of them, called

---

19 "Fellaheen" is a unique term used to refer to the farmers of Egypt.

Pishoi, was the personal attendant of the bishop and had been with him at the house of Guirguis. He welcomed them most cordially and saw to it that their baggage was safely placed on the cart. Then, each mounted a donkey and started for the bishopric.

Pishoi entertained them on the road by pointing to them the boundaries of the bishopric estate and naming all the family chiefs who lived on it, as well as describing the different breeds of cattle and crops growing thereon. His accounts were so interesting that before they knew it, they found themselves entering the garden gate. It was a simple wooden door with a big cross inlaid on its center, but overhead was an arch on which a sweet scented creeper grew lusciously. As Guirguis passed beneath that arch, he took a quick observant glance at the whole garden. It was well-tended and very trimmed, though some parts of it seemed a little wild. At its farthest end was a great big sycamore beside which flowed a canal. He turned to Pishoi and said, "Your garden is a lovesome thing."

Pishoi answered, "You shall find it more lovesome when you become familiar with it. But now we must hasten to the mansion, for Abba Moussa is waiting for you."

The mansion was simple. It was a two-story square edifice with a white verandah running all around it, roofed and balustraded with arches. Only three steps led to it. By the walls were the usual mastabas covered with cushions. The door of the mansion stood ajar, and the four walked into a spacious rectangular hall, well-lit and airy because of a wide colored glass dome in the midst of its ceiling. Each of the two longer sides were shortened by a row of six pillars. It evidently served as the reception room, for it was well-furnished. Pishoi led them to the right, and passing between the pillars, he went three more steps, and pushed a door gently. They walked into a well-sized living room, to the right of which was a half-open door on which Pishoi knocked. Being told to go in, he ushered the guests into the presence of the man of God.

He came forward to meet them with open arms, and before Guirguis could bend down to kiss his hand, he had enfolded him within his arms saying, "I am so very happy to see you, my son, and I can see that you are well." Then, when he had saluted each in turn, he asked how their journey was and whether they wanted to wash or change their clothes. Receiving an answer in the negative, he said, "Well then, I will meet you immediately in the church where we will offer the prayer of Thanksgiving."[20]

They all walked out into the garden, passed behind the mansion and into a footpath lined with palm trees on either side that led up to the church door. Here, the bishop paused to point out the intricate lacy designs carved on the door, interspersed with crosses. Then he added, "When we finish our prayers, I will tell you the history of this church."

They all went in, walked up to the iconostasis, knelt down to kiss the floor, then stood up and repeated out loud the Lord's Prayer, the Prayer of Thanksgiving, and Psalm 51. After that, they recited the Third Hour. At the end, the bishop gave them the blessing. They sat down in silence for a few minutes. Then Abba Moussa said, "Now I suggest that you have a close view of the church. If you care to ask any

---

20 The prayer of Thanksgiving is the first prayer recited in every occasion. It is said before every prayer hour of the Agpeya, at the start of the Vespers, Matins, and Liturgy, and during the Sacraments.

questions, I will be too glad to answer them. If you would rather get acquainted with the mansion and its adjoining buildings and examine the church later on, you can do that too. I want you to know that you are here free to do what pleases you, and I hope you can consider me as a father and come to me with all of your requests and questions."

Guirguis answered, "If we did not consider you more than a father, we would not have accepted your hospitality so eagerly. As for our freedom, we know that with you we can be perfectly free. Right now, we would really like to know all about the church, don't we, Shenouti?" Shenouti assented.

So they were left to look closely at the different parts of the church for as long as they wanted. Having finished their study, they returned to the bishop and asked, "Who is the Saint unto whom this church is dedicated?"

"It is called after Abba Moussa."[21]

"Abba Moussa? But that is surely you, Abouna!"

The bishop smiled benignantly and said, "No, my boys. It is Abba Moussa the strong. He is one of the outstanding figures of our church."

"Please tell us about him." So they all sat down, and the revered bishop related to them the story of Abba Moussa, known as "the strong."

---

[21] Abba Moussa, known in the west as St. Moses the Black or the Strong, is a beloved desert father of the Coptic Church. Born in the fourth century A.D., he started his life as a slave, and later as a ruthless vagabond. His conversion to Christianity is one of the greatest examples of repentance in Church history His feast day is commemorated on Baounah 24, or July 1 on the Gregorian calendar..

ΠΙⳆⲱⲢⲒ ⲈⲐⲨ   ⲀⲂⲂⲀ ⲘⲰⲤⲎ

St. Moses the Strong

***

Pishoi was then charged to show Guirguis and Shenouti the quarter reserved for the guests, built at the back of the Mansion. From the big hall which they entered, they passed into a short corridor leading to a spacious court on which opened several rooms. These rooms were reserved for the many guests who always came to visit Abba Moussa. The two lads were given a room of their choice. They were left alone after being told that from one o'clock upwards, they can ask for their lunch.

Guirguis asked, "Are we to have our meals with Abba Moussa?"

"Oh yes. The holy father always likes to keep his guests company—unless they want to be alone."

"Very good! Then we'll make good use of this advantage."

***

The two lads spent the first few days scouring every nook and cranny and making acquaintances with everybody. By the end of the first week, they had not only become familiar with the people and the place, but had made friends with the different beasts, too: the horses, the donkeys, the cows, and the cattle. They all welcomed them as they made their way from the garden into the fields. Guirguis's favorite was a year-old blackjack charger of very high spirits, which he called Meshir. Every morning, soon after sunrise, Guirguis would run to the steeple and have a ride on Meshir. Shenouti would run out with Guirguis, but he did not mind which animal he mounted—a horse, a donkey, or even a mule. The two lads would set out together, but neither Guirguis nor Meshir were in a mood to keep pace with Shenouti and his mount, and would soon be galloping at top speed leaving the latter to his own pace.

After the ride, Guirguis and Shenouti would have their breakfast out in the open, either in the garden under the mighty sycamore, or in the field by some canal, or one of the houses of the fellahin. They saw Abba Moussa at lunch and at dinner, but they were told from the first day that should either of them want to see the bishop any hour of the day, they could just walk into his room. Being an old man, he did not go out except rarely. To make up for his inability to go on his pastoral visits, he gave his people free access to his room at all times, morning and night.

On the third day of their arrival, Guirguis and Shenouti walked in at lunch time with a big bunch of grapes, for which they had climbed the vine. When they gladly offered it, Abba Moussa said, "Grapes have been a symbol used by the church since the earliest times. But it has some especially beautiful associations for us Copts."

Guirguis broke in, "Do tell us some of them."

Abba Moussa smiled his calm benignant smile and said, "But that is just what I was going to do, my boy! It was a bunch of grapes which was the sign of one of our saintliest patriarchs. You see, the holy Patriarch Yulianus, the eleventh in succession to St. Mark,[22] lay ill one day, and

---

22 St. Mark the Evangelist is the founder of Christianity in the land of Egypt. He is also the first Pope of the Coptic Church, and every succeeding Patriarch sits in the See of St. Mark.

he saw a vision of an angel appearing to him and telling him that early next morning, a young vinedresser would come to ask about bringing the first fruits of his labor. He was to be declared the successor to the people. The next day, the man came in with his bunch of grapes as was foretold; the Patriarch took his hand and said to all those around him, 'This is your father after me; he is elected by the Lord.' Seeing their questioning eyes, he added, 'My race is nearing its end,' then related to them his dream. Soon afterwards, the holy father departed in peace unto the Blessed Savior, and the people took the vinedresser and made him their Patriarch. This vinedresser is Saint Demetrius, the twelfth Patriarch to sit on the chair of St. Mark. He is the one who calculated for us our computation for the Resurrection Feast date,[23] even though at his election he barely knew how to read and write. Read his biography in the history of the patriarchs, that you may know the holy fathers of the Blessed Church, who have been a beacon illuminating the darkness of nations, as well as of individuals."

Guirguis asked, "Why don't you tell us his life story, so that it will be doubly edifying?"

Abba Moussa was silent for a bit, then said, "Maybe one evening, I will tell it to you from beginning to end. For now, I must finish my meal, for I am awaiting some of my children who are coming for advice and guidance."

"Alright, father. Maybe when you are free you will send for us. We should like to hear more of the associations with

23 Pope Demetrius recruited the help of scientists to create the Apakty formula, which determines the feast of the Resurrection to be the Sunday following the full moon after the vernal equinox and Passover. This was approved by the Council of Nicea, but Pope Gregory later decided to change the date formulation. As a result, the Western and Eastern churches tend to celebrate the Resurrection on different dates.

St. Demetrius

the grapes."

"I think I have enough time to tell you a very touching incident: Abba Macarius,[24] father of the Western desert monks, was ill one summer day. One of his children brought to him a bunch of grapes to refresh him. The great saint thought that the very old hermit living a few paces away from him was more in need of the grapes, and thus sent them to him. The very old hermit thought to himself, 'There is a young man who had recently come to the desert, he is more in need of refreshment because he is still young and untempered,' and he sent the bunch to him. The young man thought someone else more in need, and so the bunch of grapes passed from one brother on to another, none knowing from where it had come until it came back to Abba Macari. The great saint gave thanks to the Heavenly Father for the love which filled the hearts of the brethren for one another, to the extent that each thought of someone else. May their blessings be with us all."

***

On Sundays, the two lads would attend the Holy Service in the Church. It was the only day on which they neither went out for a ride, nor had their breakfast. The Service started very early, so that by nine o' clock it was over. It was very interesting to sit and listen to the conversations that took place while they all sat for breakfast, in accordance with the Apostolic tradition. Usually, chairs were brought

---

24 St. Macarius, known as the "Great" or the "Egyptian" (not to be confused with St. Macarius of Alexandria and St. Macarius the Bishop), is a great desert father of the fourth century. His feast day is commemorated on Baramhat 25, or April 3.

just outside the church door, but if it was too hot or too cold, the visitors were led to the spacious reception hall of the mansion.

It was the third Sunday since Guirguis and Shenouti arrived. They were sitting for lunch. Guirguis said, "It is a real delight to hear your sermons, holy father. You always manage to make them short, clear and to the point, while never frightening the listeners with the horrors of hell or the punishments of God, as some fathers do."

Abba Moussa laughed in his childlike manner and said, "The Blessed Apostle said that 'love casts out fear.'[25] The righteous Abba Antony,[26] father of monks, was once asked if he was afraid of God. He immediately answered, 'No,' to the astonishment of the questioner who then asked, 'How is that?' The righteous saint answered, 'Because I love Him, and where there is love, there is no fear.' I always remind myself of this saying whenever I get up to speak, and then every thought of punishment and horror disappears from my mind."

Shenouti asked, "Then why shouldn't all the fathers remember that, instead of just doing their best to portray the Loving Father as a bogey?"

Abba Moussa stroked his beard slowly then said, "I am sorry that many of us dwell on the awfulness of God more than His love. But don't let that upset either of you. Don't we always say in the Liturgy, 'No speech is ever able to define

---

25 1 John 4:18.

26 Known as St. Anthony the Great, or the Egyptian, he is a fourth-century saint and the founder of monasticism. His feast day is Tobi 22, or January 30.

the ocean of Your love for Man,'[27] and don't we always refer to God as 'the Lover of Man?'

"Yes!" exclaimed the two boys together.

Just then, one of the attendants came in. Walking up to Abba Moussa, he whispered to him a few words, at which the bishop answered out loud in apparent delight, "Excellent!" He then turned to Guirguis and asked, "Do you know your cousins from Samanoud?"[28]

Guriguis shook his head but added, "I have heard about them a great deal from dear cousin Mariam."

"Well," said the bishop, "you shall have the pleasure of seeing them shortly. The courier has just arrived from Babylon,[29] but the horse is faster than the sailboat, as you know well."

"Is the whole family coming?"

"No. The father and mother will be staying with dear Mariam. Youannis, Mena, and Demiana will come here alone. The courier says that they left Babylon yesterday. The time of their arrival will depend on the wind. Therefore, be on the lookout."

Guirguis was very delighted to hear this and said, "I'm glad that that at last, Mariam's sister managed to go and stay with her for sometime. I was a little worried about her when

---

27 From the Liturgy of Saint Gregory the Theologian.

28 Samanoud was one of the sites at which the Holy Family stayed, and therefore became of great importance to the believers. It is 121 kilometers northeast of Cairo.

29 Babylon here refers to what is now known as "Coptic Cairo" or "Old Cairo." It was thus called since 701 B.C., when the Prophet Jeremiah and some of his friends fled from the captivity decreed by King Nebuchadnezzar. It is also referred as the "Coptic Quarter" or "Al-Fustat" in this novel.

I first came because it was the first time I left her." At those words, he fell silent for a few seconds and seemed to have suddenly been transferred into another world. Abba Moussa watched him very tenderly, leaving him to his reverie as he usually did whenever he saw him in his faraway mood.

The lad came to with the same suddenness with which he had floated away, then said a little wistfully, "I shall be glad to meet these cousins of mine. Big Brother told me a great deal about them, saying that their father is of sterling worth. He described their house in Samanoud, and the joyful days which he spent there when he went to wed cousin Mariam. He also told me what a very dignified and highly honored man their grandfather was. Big Brother had promised to take me to Samanoud this summer. Now I shall meet them just as he said—but how different are the circumstances!"

Guirguis was again on the point of floating away, but he brought himself back briskly by rising from his place and going to Abba Moussa, whose hand he took and kissed most warmly saying, "Forgive me, holy Father. I am very happy to be with you, and very happy also that I shall meet my cousins for the first time in your abode, for you are almost..."

He cut his sentence short, but the old bishop patted him on the shoulders very tenderly and said, "It is delightful for me to be told that I am almost Big Brother to you, for I know how deeply you love him, and I know what a man he was."

Guirguis again kissed the bishop's hand, and the bishop clasped the young lad's hand firmly within his for a few seconds murmuring, "May God comfort and strengthen you, and repose the soul of Big Brother." Then letting go of his hand, Guirguis went back to his seat. The conversation for the rest of lunch centered on the cousins of Samanoud.

***

When the cousins anchored at Wissim at four o'clock that afternoon, Guirguis and Shenouti were on the quay with Pishoi, who duly introduced them to each other. The young people hailed each other most eagerly and were openly delighted in this long-sought encounter. They clasped each other's hands most warmly and decided to go on foot to the Mansion in order to have a longer time on the road. Only Demiana was given a donkey for the ride, which was led by Shenouti.

The eldest of the cousins was Youannis, a lad of sixteen, of a very serious mien. He had a high forehead, deep-set eyes, an almost aquiline nose, thick lips, and a heavy jaw. Even at that early age, he pondered and deliberated and spoke in measured tones. He was of medium height, but heavily built. His brother Mena, on the other hand, was taller and thinner. He had the same high forehead, but his eyes were not deep-set; rather, they were big, frank eyes. His nose was straight, but he had the same thick lips and heavy jaw. In contrast to his brother, he was both impetuous and impulsive. Their sister Demiana was as slender as a reed. She had a face that could have been that of a pharaonic queen, only in different attire. There was a softness—a daintiness—a somewhat indefinable quality of grace about her which won all hearts, and she bore herself like a queen, though she was not quite twelve.

The road was passed only too quickly by the group of

young people. They had not finished their talking when they found themselves suddenly before the mansion. Guirguis asked them if they had the marvelous opportunity of meeting Abba Moussa before, to which they all answered in the affirmative.

"But it is the first time we come here," said Yoannis.

"Well," answered Guirguis, "then I shall introduce you to all the little nooks and crannies which Shenouti and I have been to, and you shall find that staying here is a grand adventure."

He had barely finished his words when they all saw Abba Moussa coming out onto the verandah with some guests. He seated the guests and came to meet the young arrivals, welcoming them most heartily, and asking them about everyone at home. Then he said, "I am sorry, I have to attend to my other guests. Guirguis, you lead your cousins to the guests' quarters and let them choose the rooms they like. Then you can entertain yourselves until dinner time, when I shall be with you." With these words, the bishop left.

Guirguis led his cousins to his room first, then showed them the rest of the rooms, of which they chose one which was especially big. Shenouti assisted Pishoi in arranging the luggage, while Demiana supervised and the boys watched. When everything was put in its place, Guirguis addressed Demiana saying, "Are you tired, or shall we go out for our first round of inspection?"

Mena answered, "She can stand a great deal. Do you think she is fragile?"

Guirguis laughed. "Lord, no! But ladies do need to have some rest, don't they? I never had the luck of having a sister, but dear Mariam always told me that."

Youannis added, "Yes Guirguis, Aunt Mariam is right. But Demiana is a healthy 'little' girl, and she is accustomed to be in the open for long stretches. You see, she never had the luck of having a sister, either. And having only brothers, she got used to being about, though she is not a tomboy."

"Alright, then" said Guirguis, "Let's go out. I am sorry to have lost so much time before starting."

Youannis answered, "Don't be sorry for being courteous."

So off they started. Of course, the first place they went to was the church. Both Guirguis and Shenouti told them all that they had learned about the place, each complementing the other's narrative.

When they finished what they had to say, they all said the Lord's Prayer aloud, crossed themselves, then walked out into the garden. There, they sauntered leisurely for a while. Then Guirguis told them about Meshir, and they said they would like to see him.

Mena added, "Even Demiana is an able rider, though very few girls are given the freedom to ride."

Guirguis was more than delighted to hear that, and shook hands with Demiana very cordially. They then went to the stable.

Meshir was delighted to see Guirguis, who patted him saying, "You have to be very careful with Demiana when she gets on your back, Meshir my friend. She is not fragile, but she is certainly dainty." Then he asked her, "Have you ever ridden a very tempestuous steed, Demiana?"

She examined Meshir very closely, and putting her hand

on his muzzle, she answered, "Once, I nearly killed myself riding on a very wild one."

"Good God, we don't want you to kill yourself!" said Guirguis.

She smiled a most radiant smile saying, "No, no. I won't do that. I don't suppose Meshir—with all his fiery temper—will hurt me, for I think that we have already taken a liking to each other, haven't we Meshir?" She gave him a gentle pat, to which the horse responded by putting his muzzle close to her cheek. She led Meshir out and had a short gallop with him, to the great enjoyment of Guirguis.

They remained outdoors until sunset. It was a most gorgeous one, and they watched it from under the mighty sycamore tree. Then they went in for a little rest.

At dinner, all promptly came in. Contrary to his habit, Abba Moussa was a little late. He excused himself, stating that since they had last seen him in the afternoon, the flow of people did not cease, and so he was kept later than he expected.

Youannis said, "Holy father, you don't need to apologize."

Abba Moussa's tender smile lit up his whole face as he asked, "Why not?"

"Well, first of all, you are an elder, a prelate of the church."

"Is that a good enough reason for a man to be inconsiderate?"

"Nay, not inconsiderate. But we all know that you are a very busy man. You have your own mission to perform, and you have to bear the burden of so many people."

"My son, pray that God may give me grace to enable me to be really worthy of performing my mission. As to the burdens of others, each of you bears other people's in his own measure, and I hope by God's grace that such bearing of other's burdens will grow with you as you grow."

The bishop's eyes were aglow as he spoke, looking at his young guests, but as they rested on Guirguis, there was a deeper insight and sympathy in them. The young lad responded spontaneously to the old man's compassion and deep inspiration. He continued, "If we survey the great people, who by God's grace have adorned our church and set for us a pattern of Christian charity, we shall find that our burdens, however heavy, grow lighter by their inspiration."

"Do tell us some of their stories, holy father," entreated Guirguis.

So the conversation centered around the history of the church, and how the fathers laid firm its foundation by their life and by their martyrdom. When dinner was over, the young people, still eager to hear more stories from Abba Moussa, asked if they could stay a little longer. So they were taken into the Bishop's private reception room, where they remained until it was nearly midnight. He recounted to them incident after incident from the lives of different saints, both men and women. Then he said, "Having mentioned the bearing each other's burdens, I shall tell you of an incident which happened in one of St. Pakhomius's monasteries[30] to conclude tonight's stories:

---

30   St. Pakhomius (292-348) was an Egyptian desert father, and the founder of cenobitic monasticism. His feast day is the 14th of Bashans, or May 22.

"A young man went to Abba Pakhomius and confessed to him that he was a prodigal and asked if he could become a monk. The great St. Pakhomius accepted him, giving him special rules by which to abide to make up for his past waywardness. The young man accepted, and for some time, everything went on very well. Then the young man again committed the same error which he had confessed before, and instead of going to Abba Pakhomius and telling him of it, he kept silent, thinking he will not be discovered. But that great saint was well-versed in the knowledge of human souls. By the Grace of God, he could discern by the spirit many of the unconfessed sins. He was watching that wayward brother very closely and knew that something wrong had happened. It pained him that the young man did not confess, for this was a sign of unreadiness for repentance. He meditated long on how to deal with this young man whom he wanted to save. At first, he thought of sending him away from the monastery for sometime, but desiring to save him from humiliation, he found it better to send him after several brothers to another monastery of his to await him there.

A few days later, the elder set out very early to go and see how they had fared. It just so happened that on the eve of his arrival, the young sinner, praying at night, was roused by his own conscious to confess. So when the great saint did arrive the next day, the young man sought an audience to whom he confessed with tears his failings, and concluded by saying, 'Now I lay myself at your mercy, and I accept whatever judgment you pass on me.' Abba Pakhomius then asked him to withdraw so that he may ponder the matter out. Then he called on one of the men he had sent with this young man. He was a very saintly old father called Surial who had

ПΙΑΓΙΟC
ΑΒΒΑ ΠΑϢΜ
ST. PAKHOM

KOINO
NIA

led a spotless life. Having told him the story of the young man and asking him to keep the secret he said, 'I have told you his story because I know that a man such as him must live with someone else for a few years in order to conquer his own feelings. If you are willing to take him under your guidance and let him stay with you day in and day out until he has conquered, I will let him stay. If not, I have to dismiss him. I know this is a difficult thing to ask of you because you have lived for years in utter seclusion, and because you will have to fight for this young man's salvation—a fight that will be quite costly to you.'

The old Surial answered calmly, 'The Lord Jesus Christ grant me the grace to fight this young man's fight, and help him out of his own shortcomings. It will be difficult as you say, but this is certainly a grand privilege to be able to lead one soul to salvation, for this is the road our Good Savior laid out for us.'

At these words, St. Pakhomius called the young man and said, 'I shall let you stay. Henceforth, this dear old man Surial will be your father. You shall live with him in his cell. All I ask of you is to obey him implicitly.' So the young man lived in the cell of Surial for nine years. The old man strove with him, guiding him, praying with and for him, training him to be one of 'God's Athletes,' until he won him to the way of peace and set him on his feet. And now my children, good night."

Guirguis got hold of Abba Moussa's hand and kissed it saying, "Just one thing before you leave. Do you remember the story of the two monks you related to us the other day? Please repeat it to us tonight, then we will leave you in peace."

The bishop patted Guirguis on the back and said, "Alright, my boy."

Youannis remonstrated, "You have had a taxing day, and we have already taken a good deal of your time. Maybe the story can be told on some other occasion."

"No, no," replied Abba Moussa, "for your sakes, I will it tell now:

"Once, two of the brethren went into the city to sell the work of their hands, distribute the money among the needy, and go back to their monastery. They parted company, that each may do his deeds of charity in secret. While apart, one of the two fell into sin. When they met, the sinner said, 'I can't go back to the monastery, for I have sinned.' The other, desiring to save his brother, answered promptly, 'I, too, have sinned. But didn't our Good Savior say that He came not to call the righteous, but sinners unto repentance?'[31] Reminding his brother of those whose repentances were accepted, he convinced him to go back with him. The two returned together and went immediately to their Abbott, confessing to him their sins. He gave each of them penance for three days, praying for them in the meanwhile. Then it was revealed to him by the Spirit that only one of them had sinned, and that God accepted his penance for sake of his brother who did not sin, but instead took the sin of his brother."

As the bishop ended, they all stood up to go, but the elder said, "Wait, I have something to add for Youannis, who thought that you have already taken too much of my time:

---

31   Luke 5:32.

"A young monk lived near an old father, and whenever the young man was puzzled or in temptation, he ran to the cell of the old father. Then for several days, he did not come near the old father's cell, so that the elder was forced to go to him to ask him why he had stopped coming.

The young man said, 'I was somewhat ashamed of myself for taking so much of your time and energy.'

The old father smiled, then pointed to a lit candle asking, 'Have you any other candles?'

'Oh yes my father.'

'Bring them all to me.'

The young man obeyed. When all the candles were brought, he was told to light them all from one lit candle.

The the old father asked, 'Has the light of the first candle grown any less for lighting all these?' 'No,' answered the young man.

'Then,' replied the father, 'come to me as often as you want, for it will be a great advantage to me if my candle can kindle another, for then there will be more light.'"

They all shook and kissed the hand of Abba Moussa as they walked out. He kept Youannis to the end saying, "This was just for your edification, my son. A young man like you who is meant to be a leader among his people, and who will have to bear heavy responsibilities, must be trained very early on and be edified thereby." He clasped the young man's hand firmly within his, putting his other hand on his shoulder, and looking him straight in the face with his glowing eyes.

Youannis smiled quite contentedly answering, "Why,

yes, holy father, you certainly have the right to reprimand, and no apology."

"The right of fatherly love and responsibility," he patted the young man's shoulders. "The Grace of God abide with you, my son."

***

Once a month, on a Friday, a group of monks from a different monastery in the vicinity would come to spend the day with Abba Moussa, questioning him and discussing their problems. They came very early in the morning, attended the church service, then remained in church for the rest of the morning for these meetings. Laymen, who so desired, could also attend these meetings. Guirguis and his cousins took advantage of these meetings.

The discussion at one of these meetings was of great interest to Guirguis. A young monk was asking about the significance of the prayers of the departed.

Abba Moussa said, "As Christians, we believe in eternal life, and therefore, in the existence of those who depart this world. When they do depart, they retain their personalities, otherwise, they would be nonexistent. So long as they retain their personalities, they are surely interested in our welfare. Nay, they are more interested in us, for they have gone on to a higher place. Thus, the bond between them and us remains, so we pray for them and they pray for us."

The same young monk said, "But once we leave this body, we lose the chance of being forgiven, don't we?"

Abba Moussa crossed himself, then spoke very slowly, "How can we limit God's mercy? We call Him, 'Father of all mercies and Lord of all comfort.'[32] We know that He gave us His Only-Begotten Son to save us. We are told by the saints of the church that Man may be able to count the grains of sand on all the seashores and number the stars in heavens, but he can never encompass God's mercy. If that is so, how can this limitless, incomparable mercy be only limited to this life?"

Other monks joined in, "But what about God's justice?"

"Oh yes, God is justice, but His measures are certainly different from ours. When we think of His justice, we must remember three things: First, that His mercy is infinite; second, that He gave to each of us different talents and, therefore, will demand from each of us according to whatever talents were given, so that a one-talent man who strove to the best of his ability will certainly be more commendable than a ten-talent man who strove for only nine talents; and third, that He made each one of us a keeper of his brother through prayer. You should know that prayer is not merely lip service, nor is it even fervor; it is a mighty battle. 'Unto Thee have I lifted up my soul,'[33] cried the Psalmist, and certainly, lifting up one's souls to God's height is a mighty task, mightier still when it is done for someone else's sake. All those who have earnestly prayed know what battles they have waged in their prayers. Hence, when we pray for our bother who has sinned, the price of spiritual warfare is paid, but not necessarily by the sinner. God has created us brothers, and as such, keepers of each other, and therefore, bearers of each

---

32 From the absolution of the third hour prayer in the Agpeya.

33 Psalm 25:1.

other's burdens. Our prayers for the departed are two-sided: Those higher up—'those just men made perfect'[34]—pray for us that God may give us grace to carry on the struggles here below; as for us here on earth, we plead for God's mercy. Those in heaven pray for us—and cannot but do that—for they are our 'big brothers.'"

Here, Abba Moussa paused, and his eyes sought Guirguis who sat there as one in a trance, his whole face ablaze. Then he continued, "And big brothers are always concerned for their younger brothers. Thus, in our Liturgy, after mentioning the names of the saints, we say, 'We, oh our Lord, are not worthy to pray for them, but they who are standing before the throne of the Only-Begotten Son intercede for us.' We pray for them—though we are younger and weaker—by that bond of solidarity which cements us all together. Thus, the prayer is mutual, and both sides are lifted up by it. Didn't St. Paul often ask the newly converted to pray for him? Thus prayer strengthens the tie that binds our hearts in Christian love; it is the inevitable outcome."

A short interval of silence ensued. It seemed as though the "big brothers" spoken of by the saintly man were present in their midst. Abba Moussa broke the silence in his quiet manner, asking if there more questions. The discussions, however, did not last very long after that, for presently, the querying voices ceased. At that, Abba Moussa stood up and asked them all to stand and say the Lord's Prayer in unison. His eyes were still on Guirguis, who rose up with the rest and prayed with them, though he had not quite come back from his reverie which he had been in since he heard the words "Big Brother" uttered by the Bishop.

---

34 Heb. 12:23.

The holy man gave them the benediction and they all went out, save Guirguis who remained in his seat. When they had all gone out, he went to the Bishop, took his hand, and kissed it most fervently saying, "How can I describe to you my state of ecstasy caused by your talk?"

The Bishop seated him, put an arm around his shoulder, and said very tenderly, "Don't try to describe it to me, my lad. I have been watching you, and I have seen your face— nay, your whole frame. Maybe I know what you have been experiencing. Such experiences are best unuttered."

The young man clasped the old man's hand within his for a few seconds, then again kissed it as the two rose up. They stood facing the sanctuary in silence for a while, then Abba Moussa said, "The grace of God abide within you, and may the blessings of the Holy Virgin and all the saints be with you." Then they both went out.

The tables were set for lunch, and those present were seated, awaiting their host. When he arrived, they all rose up. He came to his seat, lifted up his arms in blessings and prayer, then sat down. The rest followed suit. Although Guirguis was neither a clergyman nor the oldest one present, he was seated at the right hand of the Bishop, a place accorded to him by the consent of all those present for the sake of Big Brother, whom they all knew.

They ate with a light heart, talking of the wonders God performs with them through His saints, and how He keeps them as He kept Daniel in the lion's den. Then, just as the meal was ending, a young monk asked whether elders had the right to punish youngsters for the sake of discipline. Abba Moussa deflected the question to the group, leaving them to debate the matter for a while. Then he said, "When we love, then we have the right to chastise, following the pattern of God. Do you remember what the great Abba Macarius said in answer to that very question? He said, 'If you feel an inward satisfaction in punishing someone, refrain immediately, for then you are not disciplining, you are revenging. But if your heart is bleeding while you are punishing, then you can do it, for then you aim to reform.'"

When the meal was over, they were all left to do whatever they pleased. At sunset, they all gathered once more for prayer, after which the monks returned to their monastery.

The young people stayed at Wissim for the whole summer. The days would be cherished within their hearts for the rest of their lives. They were all filled with peace and a sense of well-being. They made several excursions to the nearby places and monasteries within the region. Oftentimes, after their ramblings, they would sit underneath the mighty sycamore and listen to stories about Big Brother. Guirguis would also ask his cousins to tell him of their home in Samanoud, and told them how Big Brother had promised to take him there that very summer. Thus the bond of friendship cemented their bond of blood.

***

The eleventh of September was a very exciting day, for it was the New Year. On the preceding evening, the little boys went about chanting the folk songs of the day. Some of them carried the first fruits of the earth, such as dates and pomegranates, offering them to passers-by. Others carried grain stalks and weaved them into different shapes,

ⲡⲓⲛⲓϣϯ
ⲃⲃⲁ ⲙⲁⲕⲁⲣⲓ

THE GREAT
ABBA MACARIUS

hanging them on the door posts of their friends as a wish of abundance for the coming year. As the darkness came, they lit lanterns and went about chanting more songs.

The following day, everyone went to church early, where the Liturgy and the prayers of the day were sung. The service ended at nine. All those present were offered breakfast by the bishop, who went about greeting them one by one and asking how each one was faring. After breakfast, they all went out into the fields, where each picked up their favored fruits. Some gathered in groups by the banks of the Nile to chant the folk songs, while others took a dip in the river. It was indeed the New Year, the day on which they celebrated the inundation of the river that was sacred to their forefathers, and still remained for them a symbol of God's ceaseless bounty. When the sun was high up in the heavens, everyone went home. In the evening just before the sunset, they regathered by the banks of the Eternal River, and once more chanted their songs. There were young lads who performed some acts, horses danced to the sound of the pipes and the drums, while some men displayed their dexterity at fencing. To end it all, bonfires were lit. After that, the prayer of the twelfth hour was sung, and everyone went home.

Guirguis and his cousins still loitered under the mighty sycamore when all the people had gone, recounting to each other some of the day's adventures. Abba Moussa soon came to them saying, "My children, it is time for you to go to bed. You have had quite an exciting day, but you must wake up early tomorrow to journey home."

Here, Mena said, "Sometimes I wish that time would stop for a short while to leave us enjoy the hour."

The old man smiled most sympathetically and said, "We all do, my boy, but that is not the decree of our Heavenly Father. He wants life to move forward, thus offering the chance to grow in wisdom—or rather, the chance to be renewed. For everyday is a fresh beginning, a new hope."

Mena answered, "True, holy father, but we would only like to capture the joy of the moment and keep it a little longer, if possible."

"We can keep it in our memory, my lad, and treasure it in times of stress."

Youannis came a little forward and said to his brother, "Though what you say is true, and we would love to remain awake all night, if possible, yet, we must obey our dear father."

With these words, all of them walked towards the Mansion with Abba Moussa in their midst. They walked arm-in-arm, very slowly. The holy father, pointing to the beautiful sky and telling them the names of some of the stars said, "The Heavens declare the glory of God, and the firmament showeth His handiwork."[35]

***

Next morning, they were all up early. After attending the service, they had their breakfast as usual. After eating, Youannis, Mena, and Demiana took their leave of Abba Moussa. Guirguis and Shenouti walked with them as far as the river, then commended each other to God's care. Thus

---

35 Psalm 19:1

they parted, promising to come back the following summer, if possible.

Guirguis and Shenouti remained three more days at Wissim, after which they, too, started for home. Guirguis lingered for a few minutes by the side of Abba Moussa, holding his hand and looking at the wide expanse of the field and sky. The old man put his free arm around the lad's shoulder saying, "God be with you, my boy, and may you grow up to realize all the hopes centered on you." Guirguis kissed his hand in silence, then he and Shenouti were soon on their way home.

***

The following summer, Guirguis took Shenouti and went to Wissim. This time they were joined by Mena and Demiana only. Youannis was on tour to various provinces to stay with different people. His father thought such a tour would give him firsthand knowledge of the state of the Copts—how they were living, what provinces had more freedom, where were the influential ones among them, and whether there were any complaints.

Youannis, being the eldest of the governor of Samanoud, was singled out by his people for leadership, and they did their best to cultivate within him the necessary traits for such a role. He possessed that which enabled him to realize the dreams of his parents: his well-balanced nature and his deep thinking, coupled with courage and the power to face the truth even if it was against him. All these were part of his personality and helped him to be a leader. Hence this summer, he started on his tour to the provinces, a tour lasting eighteen months, for he stopped in each central town long enough to gather the necessary information. Thus, he gathered the knowledge and started the friendships which were to be of use in later years.

Consequently, Mena and Demiana went alone to Wissim. Mena was especially sent to Wissim for a purpose—that of starting his study of medicine. For within the monastery was an old and experienced monk who had expert knowledge of all the herbs and their uses, and had effected cures which were well-nigh miraculous. Mena, who wanted to be a doctor, was counseled by Abba Moussa to come and seek learning at the hands of this old monk. So that summer, he merely slept at the bishopric; nay, he even spent some of his nights at the monastery. Thus Guirguis and Demiana, followed by the ever faithful Shenouti, were alone most of the time.

***

The young girl, in spite of her tender years, possessed marvelous powers of insight and sympathy. She could sit and listen for hours while Guirguis talked to her. Most of these meetings were under the mighty sycamore. Shenouti would be always within calling distance. The two would sit under that big tree, which had listened to many a tale of joy and sorrow, and seen many generations of human beings come and go. They usually went to it in the evening, having had their romping and their caroling during the day. They would sit and watch the sunset and listen to the evensong chanted by the birds in the open and by the human beings within the church. At times, the quietness of the atmosphere pervaded their souls, and they would sit in utter silence with their backs to the tree and their hands clasped. Other times, they would be bubbling over some story or some adventure. Once in a while, they would be joined by Mena, who would recount to them his experiments with his old teacher, expressing his admiration of the old man's alertness and willingness to teach him tirelessly for hours on end.

The couriers of Youannis reached them regularly and with great precision. His letters described to them places and people in detail. Abba Moussa always commented on these letters; he admired the orderly and dignified way in which Youannis expressed himself in writing.

Guirguis would say, "But the trouble with Youannis is that he is never impetuous; he is always so well poised, at least in appearances. And this is not natural in a young man."

The tender smile of Abba Moussa would light on Guirguis as he answered, "It may not be usual, but you know that there are exceptional people—and Youannis is one of them. Such a trait in him is an asset, not a trouble. You pass your judgement as a fiery youth, and I as an old man"

Here Guirguis cut in, "Pardon me, holy father. I know I should not cut you off, but if you are going to say 'as an old man,' then I shall protest. I don't think I have ever come across a younger 'old' man than you."

The bishop was quiet for a few seconds, his smile still radiant, and said, "But I *am* a very old man! I am already three score years and ten. Wait till you become as old as I am."

"But it would be a marvelous thing if I could stay as

young as you are—that is, if I ever manage to reach old age."

"Our lives are in our Father's hands—whether they are to be short or long does not count. What counts is the use we make of them. I know, my dear son, that those like you are always a target for the rulers; being a chief is a great responsibility and risk. Your fathers and Big Brother had paid the price manfully and with great dignity. Should you also be called upon to pay with your life, I know you will do it manfully and courageously. May the grace of the loving Father sustain us and enable us to be faithful unto the end. Nonetheless, my prayers for you are that God will grant you a long life because I know, Guirguis, that you will serve grandly."

The lad took the bishop's hand and kissed it. This year, the lad sat at the Bishop's left, giving the right to Demiana. She sat there listening, her big eyes wide as though she were listening through them as well as with her ears.

Abba Moussa turned to her and said, "Why so silent and wistful, my girl?"

She colored a little, then answered, "I don't know, holy father. Sometimes I get frightened at the tumult of my own heart. There are so many things I see and hear—so many changes—the times are very troubled. I feel as though I am in a little boat on rough seas."

Her eyes were fixed on Guirguis as she spoke, and Abba Moussa took her hand in his and said, "We are all in little boats on rough seas. We are very much like the disciples when they were tempest-tossed, and our safety lies in doing just what they did: in waking the Christ within us."

She was silent for a while, putting her other hand on the

old man's and pressing it gently. Then she said, "But couldn't Christ spare us the storm?"

"Yes, He could. He could have also evaded the cross, but He chose the steep and thorny path, and He blazed for us the trail that we may follow in His wake and prove to all the world how we can keep the torch burning by never flinching—even if we get burned ourselves."

Guirguis said, "Yes, holy father! Big Brother's last words to me were that I should carry the torch which fell from his hand."

Abba Moussa answered, "Just so, my boy, we should not pretend that it is an easy task. We should know exactly how difficult it is, then ask God to give us the grace sufficient for doing it. By His grace, and by the blessings of our Lady Saint Mary and all the saints, we will be able to stand the strain."

This time, Demiana answered, "Thank you, Father, for telling me that it is a difficult task. I was just saying that this evening, and Guirguis disagreed with me."

Guirguis laughed, and Abba Moussa said, "Guirguis is a naughty boy, that's all." The father then switched to a lighter mood, telling them some of the stories of the fellaheen.

Thus it was, that on this, as on all occasions, Abba Moussa kept his young guests serious yet joyful. He watched with great tenderness and interest the growing friendship between Guirguis and Demiana. It delighted his heart to hear each expressing their admiration for the other.

So the days passed too rapidly; Guirguis, Demiana, and Shenouti never found a day long enough for their activities. The beautiful summer nights under the open sky—whether the moon was full or not—lured them to stay up in the open air after dinner. Sometimes, as Abba Moussa was finishing a late interview or coming out to see if any of his men were still about (as his wont), he would chance upon them sitting on the verandah and scold them for staying up so late.

On one such encounter, Demiana remonstrated, "But the sky is so clear, and the stars are countless. They are most alluring."

"I agree with you, my girl, but you need to rest your body. You should not overtax it from now. Keep your body as fit and as strong as you can for the coming years."

She stood up and got hold of the bishop's hand, saying, "That is prophetic, holy father. Sometimes, it is such thoughts that disturb me."

"No, no, my daughter. Remember what we said the other day about waking up Christ to save the disciples from the storm? I say these things not to frighten, but to make you alert. Our blessed Savior said, 'Watch and pray.'[36] His grace will make us stand firm however, slippery the ground under us," added the Bishop, putting his arm around her shoulders. A great tenderness filled him as she looked up bravely into his eyes, and he looked past her into the eyes of Guirguis, which were aflame. Then he said, "You are too young for such thoughts, but it is good for a man to bear the yoke in his youth."[37]

***

---

36 Matt. 26:41.

37 Love and marriage between cousins was not considered taboo during this time. In fact, a number of Middle Easterners to this day are wedded to their cousins.

Both parents of Youannis, Mena, and Demiana came to Wissim on the seventh of September. They had been staying in Babylon with Mariam for sometime, and then they came to spend a week in Wissim to take Dimiana back with them to Samanoud. Mena was to stay behind with the old doctor monk. Guirguis had not met them before, but when he did meet them, they seemed quite familiar to them. They, in turn, welcomed him as a son, remarking that he looked very much like Big Brother—only he was growing taller and taller, and he was a little too impetuous.

They did not go about much, but were very interested in the people who lived on the estate, even the poorest among them. They also went on a visit to the monastery to make the acquaintance of the old monk who was teaching their son the lore of medicine.

Guirguis and Demiana kept them company, acting as guides to them. Whenever their company was not desired, the old sycamore tree gave them warm welcome.

When the New Year festivities were over, Demiana and her parents left. Guirguis went with them as far as the river and stood on the quay, waving them goodbye until they were out of sight. When he was still on the boat, before it set sail, Demiana held his hand firmly saying nothing. He asked, "Why so silent, dear one?"

She shrugged her shoulders and looked into the distance for a while, then turned her gaze to him and said quietly, "Something tells me we shall not meet for a long while."

"Long or short, we will be thinking of each other."

"Oh yes. In thought, we shall never part."

"And though that is not enough, we know that only a

thin veil hangs between us. The Loving Father is watching over us and has one arm around you and the other around me. This will keep us near."

"That's right!" She brightened at these thoughts and began to talk in a light mood, until the time for the boat to leave was proclaimed and they took leave of one another.

Walking back along with Shenouti, Guirguis mused for a while. Then turning towards his ever faithful attendant, he said, "Shenouti, there are many hard things we have to face in this life."

"Yes sir, but there are also very delightful things, too."

"You want to tell me to 'take the fat with the lean,' you sly one, only in a diplomatic fash-ion. Well, you're right. After all, I should be really grateful for these last two summers. They will grant me many pleasant memories and a hopeful outlook."

"Yes, indeed they will. And soon, we shall be going back too."

"We can delay no longer, for there is work ahead of us."

Seven days later, the two youths went back home, promising Abba Moussa that they will visit whenever possible, if but for a day.

CHAPTER TWO

The Bivouac of Life

"In the world's broad field of battle, in the bivouac of life, be not like dumb driven cattle. Be a hero in the strife"

—Longfellow

Six whole years passed, during which the young people saw nothing of each other. The only link was their thoughts and their couriers. In these six years, the young boys were straining themselves to attain the accomplishments necessary for the struggles awaiting their manhood. They were building themselves up, knowing that each had great responsibilities. Their brains, their moral fiber, and their expert knowledge would be their only aids, so they were busy fortifying them.

During these six years, they had grown up. Though they were still tender in years, yet they were expected to behave like fully grown men and were looked upon as such by their kin and their rivals alike—so much so, that they often had to forget the demands of their youth.

Youannis was then twenty-three. Being the eldest and the one who was to bear the family—as well as the community responsibility—he was to get married.

The courier, coming from Samanoud to Babylon one May evening, brought to Guirguis the invitation to go and attend the wedding. He was in the very same room in which Big Brother had breathed his last when he unfolded the letter and read it. Then putting it aside, he stood up and looked out of the window. He could not define the tumult within his heart even if he tried.

Was he delighted, or was he excited? Was he reminiscent? But what reminiscences? Were they of Big Brother and his descriptions of Samanoud? Or were they of Demiana? Well, in reality, they were all of these combined—a whole gamut of emotions and deep stirrings. A few minutes later, he turned around and walked up to the icon of the blessed Virgin, knelt down before it, and said his prayers silently. Then as though speaking to someone, he said aloud, "I am certainly very happy to be able to go to Samanoud at last... right now, I am a little puzzled. But I know that it will all clear up as it has in the past."

***

Two days later, Mariam, Guirguis, Shenouti, and a whole train of people set off for Samanoud. When they reached the outskirts of the town, Mena, with several members of the family and attendants, were awaiting them. The whole town seemed in festive mood. This was, after all, Youannis, the heir of the feudal lord. The season was also a festive one, for it was the week in which the church would celebrate the feast of Saint Demiana,[38] and there were many people who had come from near and far to make a pilgrimage to her shrine.

When Mena and Guirguis met, they embraced one another most warmly. Then they each looked at the other appraisingly.

Mena was the first to speak: "By the blessed Lady Demiana, you have grown tall! Good gracious, you tower over everybody! You're almost a giant!"

"Is that an asset?"

"Well, yes and no."

Guirguis did not pursue the question any further, but said, "As for you, you have become extremely handsome— you did not promise to be this handsome when I came across you years ago. But by our Lady, why these streaks of gray in your hair at this early age?"

Mena laughed. "To give me a look of scholarliness! I really don't know why. Maybe because I lived with the old monk for so long?"

Guirguis said, "I wonder what changes the others have undergone?"

Mena answered mischievously, "I suppose you mean

---

38 Saint Demiana is a beloved saint of the Coptic Church. As a young lady, she and forty other virgins lived in a convent to consecrate their lives to God. They were martyred at the hands of Diocletian on Tubah 13, or January 21. The consecration of her church is celebrated on Bashans 12, or May 20. That is the feast that is being celebrated in this context.

LADY DEMIANA
AND HER 40 FRIENDS

what change Demiana has undergone?"

"Well, if you'll have it that way, then yes. But I am also really quite eager to meet the groom."

Mena again laughed. "Very little changed. He only looks wiser and more preponderate than ever."

"And certainly more considerate."

"Sure enough."

The two were silent for a while, then Mena said, "I can see that you have learned to control yourself." Guirguis still remained silent, so Mena said, "In the name of all the saints, you astound me. If you were just as I saw you years ago, you would have asked about Demiana and flew at me for not giving you the answer right away."

Guirguis smiled faintly, "Yes Mena, I have learned how to control myself, you are right. And though I am aching to ask about her, I still hold my peace."

Mena placed his hand on Guirguis's shoulder, then said, "I shouldn't have started teasing you. All the same, I think it will be better not to tell you anything about her until you see her."

Guirguis acquiesced, then they both started questioning each other on what they did during their six years of absence. Presently, they were before the gate of the "big house," as it were called. The many attendants came out for the baggage and for the care of the sedan chairs and horses. Guirguis, who had made it a point of always serving Mariam himself, was being scolded by Mena who thought it more becoming that he should be the one to help her out of her sedan chair.

Mariam smiled angelically saying, "Mena, my boy,

there is no matter of formality between us." Then turning to Guirguis she added, "Let your cousin help me out this time."

Guirguis conceded, saying, "Only this once."

She stood beside her chair until Mena helped her out and led her up the flight of seven stairs to where his parents stood. Demiana was standing a little to the right behind her parents so that she was in full view. She had grown taller, but remained very slender and radiant like a lotus when it is just opening. She was exquisite in a deep turquoise dress with touches of pale cyclamen, the colors of the ancients. Her pitch black hair fell on her shoulders, and she wore long golden earrings. She also had a gauzy veil of turquoise hanging loosely down and covering only the back part of her head. She seemed to Guirguis like a fairy queen, so delicate and dainty. Yet, he did not rush up to her, but followed behind Mariam and stood waiting for her to salute her sister and her brother-in-law. Then he, in turn, saluted them, kissing their hands. Having done that, he went to Demiana, took her hands in both his, and kissed them one by one. While he was greeting her, the group was moving into the house, so they loitered a little behind. They stood facing each other in silent admiration. Her hands were still in his all the while.

A few minutes elapsed before she managed to find her tongue and said, "Welcome, welcome cousin Guirguis. It is indeed a joyous day to see you after so many years. The blessed Lady Demiana preserve you, you have grown big and tall!"

"A very joyous day for me, too. You have grown dazzling. You were certainly a beautiful girl, but you have exceeded yourself in beauty. It seemed to me as I came up the steps that you were not of this world."

He put his arm around her, and they followed the others in. Mariam was asking about Youannis, who had not made his appearance yet. Mena said that he was still out. They were then shown to their rooms, where they were duly bathed and anointed, then came down to the big reception hall where some of the other guests were already gathered. As Guirguis was leading Mariam, someone appeared through the doorway. It was none other than Youannis himself!

They stopped to greet him, and Guirguis said, "Great God, you look like a man of forty! Why, in the name of all the saints?"

Youannis laughed quietly and answered, "If you had seen what I saw, you would have aged like me."

"But man, you honestly take things too much to heart. You should forget the cares and worries of others for at least this week. The young bride must find a cheerful countenance before her—mustn't she?"

Demiana joined in, saying, "The young bride's smiles are enough for the two; she is so charmingly optimistic, that it is like tonic to be with her."

"Excellent," said Mariam. "Do I know her?"

"Of course you do," answered Youannis, "she is Ageya, the daughter of cousin Marcus."

"Yes, I do know her, the blessings of the saints be with her! You are a very lucky man to have her, my son. May God bless you both."

"Thank you, dear Aunt."

***

The seven days passed like a dream. There were so many people to meet; it was a joy to see how fond they all were of Youannis, and how highly they esteemed him. There were so many things to hear and ponder over that, before he knew it, Guirguis found the whole week at an end, and that it was time to go back. At the request of Mariam, he agreed to stay for three more days, the last of which they spent at the church of Lady Demiana.

During these days, Guirguis and Demiana did not see much of each other; she was so busy with the bride and the guests, and he was taken by Mena on many rounds. But on this last day, they were together the entire time. The service was private as the feast was over, so the family was alone in church. Demiana more than once caught a pensiveness on the face of Guirguis as he knelt by the altar, which made her heart ache.

On the way home, he was mostly silent riding beside her sedan chair. Every now and then, she would peep through the curtain and smile at him. Once when she did, he caught her hand and pressed it more strongly than usual.

The following day, a little after dawn, Guirguis and Mariam started off with their train. Demiana succeeded in convincing her father to permit her to accompany Mena and see them off to the outskirts of the city. All of them seemed tongue-tied, their hearts being too full for speech.

When they were nearly at the gates of the town, Guirguis said in a hushed tone, "I shall be needing all your prayers during the coming weeks, for I shall be at the crossroads."

Demiana and Mena answered simultaneously, "May the prayers of the saints be with you."

At the gate, the three of them lingered a little, shaking hands and bidding each other goodbye. Demiana said smiling, "Do you remember what you told me when we parted company last at Wissim?"

His face brightened. "What?"

She answered, "Only a thin veil hangs between us, and that the Lord Father is watching over us with one arm around you, and the other around me, which will keep us near."

He took her hand within both of his, and the laugh she loved rang out as he said, "The blessings of our Lady the Virgin, and of all saints, be with you."

"And with you," answered Demiana and Mena in one voice.

Then they took leave of each other, and Guirguis spurred on his horse to reach those ahead.

***

Two weeks later, Abba Moussa came to Babylon. He brought Meshir with him to give it to Guirguis as a present. On the second day of his arrival, he took Guirguis to the court and presented him to the new Wali,[39] for such was the purpose of his coming. He remained only for three days, as

---

39 The Wali is the Muslim governor of Egypt.

he could not stay longer, leaving Guirguis at his new post.

Within six months, Guirguis had succeeded in becoming the favorite courtier and first man of the Wali. Several elements served to make him that. His physical strength and prowess coupled with his height made him somewhat imposing. His ready wit and the endless stream of his tales impressed all hearers; he was a most charming conversationalist, able to quote all outstanding writers— even non-Christian ones. But above all, there was an air of mystery about him, for though he was a young courtier, he always wore black; and though he was always surrounded by the Wali and his Muslim court, he wore a big golden cross over his breast. He never joined in eating and drinking with the court, but always satisfied himself with the frugal meal brought to him by Shenouti. Above all, he had these reveries—moments when he seemed transported away from the world of men. He would be telling a story or a joke, then break off suddenly into silence and transportation. His hearers became convinced that he was in league with some unseen power.

Once, when asked in a derisive voice by one of the courtiers what happened to him, he answered firmly, "How dare you use this tone with me? Don't you know that I am sustained by the Unseen, and that I bear a charmed life?"

A few incidents confirmed his saying; once, as he was making his way through a crowd, a man thought of stabbing him in the back. Just as he was about to do it, Guirguis turned around suddenly, caught the extended dagger at the nick of time, and said as he laughed most derisively, "Fool, don't you know that I bear a charmed life? Here, take your dagger. Try if you would like some other time and see how true my words are." He threw the dagger to its owner disdainfully, and the man slunk away in shame.

On another occasion, a jealous courtier invited him to a cup of coffee, conniving with his slave to put some poison in his cup. Though the courtier put the poison with his own hand, yet when the coffee arrived he took his own poisoned cup while Guirguis drank the wholesome one.

Once during a festival, the whole group of courtiers went out shooting. One of them seized the chance to aim an arrow at Guirguis while he was talking to Shenouti. The arrow would have surely hit him had he not seemed to have finished his talk and turn around to join the Wali, just as the arrow whizzed past him.

Such incidents gave affirmation to his talk, and added to his prestige in the eyes of the Wali and many others. He became known as "the mysterious horseman."

A year after his entry into the court, the Wali's favorite wife became very ill. Guirguis found it an opportune chance to send for Mena in haste. Mena came as recommended, tried his skill, and succeeded. Thus, he was appointed doctor for the court. This only added to the prestige of Guirguis in the esteem of the Wali.

***

During this time, there came to Samanoud a distant cousin of Demiana's father. He came from Giza seeking her in marriage. He was a very wealthy young man and an only son to his parents. His name was Zoheir, and he had no thought except for his looks and his dress. His silken caftans and his fineries were the talk of the people.

Three days after his arrival, Demiana's father came to her room in the evening and told her Zoheir's purpose for coming.

She turned crimson saying, "He is not the man for me."

Her father patted her cheek lovingly saying, "Yes, he is not the man for you, but I am just passing on his message."

She put her arm around her father's neck and answered, "You have always been sympathetic and frank, and it is a joy to be your daughter. As for that cousin of ours, let's not talk of him anymore."

"Agreed, but please refrain from discourtesy. You have the right to refuse, but do it in a gracious manner."

"I'll try very hard father, because in all honesty, the man disgusts me."

Just then her mother came joyously into the room saying, "Good news, we have a baby grandson!"

Both Demiana and her father stood up saying, "May he be blessed." Then the three of them walked out hand in hand to see the firstborn of Youannis.

***

A few days later one evening, Demiana and her mother were sitting on the verandah when Zoheir suddenly joined them. He switched the topic of their conversation to the latest court gossip and said, "Believe it or not, Guirguis—who parades in his black robes and golden cross—has become just as loose as the rest of the courtiers."

Demiana collected herself, but added hotly, "I don't believe it."

Zoheir laughed disdainfully. "Your belief or disbelief will not change matters. Besides, you are so far away; you don't see how he struts up and down the city streets, nor do you hear what the people whisper about him."

She braved him his scorn. "They may whisper as they please; they dare not raise their voices above a whisper because they are lying cowards. Besides, you don't have the right to calumniate a man in his absence."

"I would say it to his face had he been here."

"You wouldn't! You don't have the courage for it. I think you are merely jealous of him."

Her mother put a restraining hand on her, then turning to Zoheir, she said, "It is not very kind of you to thus defame a man. Guirguis may be what you said of him and more, but we should do our best to build each other up, and not go away tearing at each other as you are doing now."

He answered, "But I am merely recounting facts."

"Facts that are not for edification are better left unsaid. The apostle advices us to think of whatsoever is pure and lovely and of good report."[40]

Before Zoheir could put in an answer, Youannis appeared. He noticed that Demiana looked very pale, but said nothing. As for Zoheir, he immediately changed the subject of the conversation.

---

40 Phil. 4:8.

Shortly after, the two men went out, leaving Demiana and her mother alone. As soon as they disappeared out of sight, Demiana burst into tears. Her mother kept silent until she finished her crying, then she said, "My darling, you should not have let yourself be upset by a scandalmonger. He obviously wanted to rouse you, and he succeeded; as soon as Youannis appeared, he shut up."

Demiana, still gasping, answered, "But why should he behave like this?"

"Well," answered her mother, "he is jealous. For one thing, Guirguis has first place in the Wali's heart. Guirguis also has your heart. Zoheir can neither attain the one nor the other."

Here, they were joined by father who immediately asked, "My darling beautiful one, what is the matter?" He sat down beside her, putting one arm around her shoulder and patting her under the chin with the other. Her mother told him what happened, to which he answered, "My darling, you should be sorry for so small a man instead of being angry at him."

She answered, "But such talk as his does not merely defame Guirguis, it is also dangerous! Suppose he goes about repeating it and convincing some people of it—that will mean a break in our line."

Her father said, "You say the truth, my girl, but if you want him to stop, you chose the wrong road. Have no fear, Guirguis is a popular hero. You should see him 'as he struts' (in Zoheir's words) in the streets. Everybody hails him and he hails everybody. Only a few petty souls agree with what Zoheir says. So have no fear. May the blessings of our Lady and all the saints be with Guirguis."

"Amen," answered the two women together.

Demiana's father continued, "Forget all that passed this afternoon and try to regain your gracious manners. I don't know how long this young man will stay with us, nor how many times you will have to keep him company, but remember always what I just told you." Demiana kissed her father and promised to obey.

Zoheir remained for ten whole days after the encounter. He rarely saw Demiana, but when he did, she managed to act according to her father's advice. When he said goodbye, she gave him a greeting of courtesy, but was greatly relieved to see him leave.

Guirguis was always regular with his letters. It was mostly concerned with matters of the state and written in a language that only Youannis could decipher. The greetings that were understandable by all were very short. This made Demiana worry at times. Whenever she spoke of him with Youannis, she was told that things were getting on fine, and that there was no need for her to worry. Yet a restlessness seemed to overpower her sometimes; she wished she could go and stay with Mena in Aunt Mariam's house, at times, if only for a day—but even her mother thought that was impossible. So she found that the best means for quieting her heart was to serve the people around her and to pray and meditate.

Thus the months slipped by. It was fifteen months since Mena's departure to Babylon when a courier arrived in haste, asking if Demiana could come for a short stay because Mena was ill and needed special care. Of course, Aunt Mariam did all she could for him, but she had so much to look after, and she was so frail. In Demiana's heart, she was thrilled at the invitation—though upset by the cause for it, hoping that it wouldn't be serious. Her parents were a little hesitant at first, but after deliberating together and with Demiana, they decided to let her go, as the change may do her good.

So receiving their blessing, she set off early next morning. When she arrived to her aunt's house, she found Mena still in bed, having caught an infection from one of his patients. For several weeks, all of Demiana's care and attention centered on him. Gradually, he pulled through, and while he was recuperating, Demiana became aware of the other people and objects in the household.

One day, she remarked to Mena how strange it was that they were in Guirguis's home, and yet they rarely saw him. Mena answered that he was very busy with the Wali. Then one afternoon, while sitting on the terrace busying herself with some work and listening to Mena's tales, she was roused by the sound of hoofs beating on the pavement. She left her work to look, and behold, Meshir was galloping off with Guirguis on his back while Zoheir galloped after him. This reminded her of the previous incident—which she had almost forgotten—and she related it to Mena.

"Fool that Zoheir is!" said Mena, "You should see how he really behaves before Guirguis, but father says don't worry."

Demiana answered, "Sometimes I can't help it. You see, to be frank with you, Mena, I am somewhat puzzled by the behavior of Guirguis."

Mena was silent for a short while, then added, "My darling, I admit that you are right to be puzzled. But take it from me, there is absolutely no reason for it."

"Then why don't you be more explicit?" she asked.

He answered, "I am sorry, I cannot be otherwise."

***

Another week passed. It was on a Friday and at midday. Demiana saw Guirguis gallop off on Meshir a short while ago. Now she heard a knock below, and peeping from behind the *mushrabiah*,[41] she saw Peshoi and felt glad.

"It's Abba Moussa's attendant. Dear old Abba Moussa has helped me out so many times." Pishoi was coming especially for her (to her delight). Abba Moussa came last night and was staying in the Patriarch's apartment on top of *Al-Muallakah* Church,[42] and would like to see her. She was overjoyed, and in a few minutes went down with Pishoi to see the holy man.

He was up on the top floor, sitting on a sofa in a corner overlooking the church. When she arrived, he greeted her very affectionately and seated her beside him, asking about everyone in her family by name. Then he said, "I have sent for you to speak with you about Guirguis." Her heart leapt, and he continued, "Go and look through the *mushrabiah* onto the church."

---

41 An oriel window enclosed in an intricate wooden latticework. It is common to see it in older Egyptian buildings.

42 *Al-Muallakah* Church is one of the most famous and oldest churches in all of Egypt. It is thought to date back to the third century, and is located in Old Cairo (Babylon). The Arabic word muallakah means "hanging;" the church is referred as such because it was built over the southern tower gate of the Babylon fortress, with its nave suspended above the passage.

She obeyed and saw Guirguis kneeling before the iconostasis, his head resting against it. She stood there watching him, while the old bishop came up to her side and laid a hand on her shoulder in silence. They saw him stand up and pass his hands lovingly over every carved cross; he seemed to be utterly lost in his adoration and in his quest after that power which gave the artists who made this iconostasis the patience, dexterity, and persistence to complete their masterpiece.

Then Abba Moussa led Demiana into a small sitting room, and seating her beside him, he said, "I shall speak of my own accord: Guirguis is offering himself unflinchingly for the sake of his people. He has managed to win the Wali's heart. But being the favorite courtier is no easy task; he has to always be on the alert with the jealousies and intrigues within the court—even the jealousies and slanders outside, and even from his own people. Above all this, the Wali himself may suddenly lose interest in him, or may suddenly remember that he is an 'infidel.' Do you remember when we spoke about Daniel and the lion's den? Well, Guirguis is here is in the lion's den—and not for a night. He is there day in and day out. Nay, sometimes he has to be with him eighteen hours on end. Only on Fridays, when the Wali goes to the mosque does he let Guirguis go. As soon as he leaves, the gallant man rushes to this old sanctuary to refresh his spirit and regain the strength necessary for the struggle. The only ones who know of this are Mariam, Youannis, and myself. Even Mena does not know the entire story. And now I thought it fit to call you here and tell you all about it because your love for him will be as a fortress to him to strengthen him. And now, I hear his footsteps coming up because I sent for him. He does not know you are here, so get behind that curtain now."

She obeyed, her heart beating so fast she could hardly steady herself. She had barely managed to hide herself when Guiguis walked in. Abba Moussa greeted him in his usual tender way and seated him beside himself. After a few questions about him and Mariam, he said, "I have a surprise for you in store," and pushed aside the curtain.

At sight of Demiana, Guirguis stood up exclaiming, "Good God above!" Abba Moussa stood up too. He took Demiana by the hand and brought her right before Guirguis, then went out of the room.

For a few seconds the two stared at each other as though dazed. Then Guirguis put his strong arms around her and enveloped her in his firm but loving grasp. She, on her part, put her head against his breast and sobbed like a little child. Then controlling herself, she said a little brokenly, "Why did you behave like this? I could chide you had I not loved you so much."

He put his hand under her chin and lifted her face up to his, looking into her eyes. Then passing his hand over her hair, he said, "It is because I love you so that I thus behaved. Did you not hear of the scandals and the looseness of Guirguis?"

She remonstrated saying, "Hush—do not speak vain words."

"I did not want you to get entangled with me. You see, for some time we shall be waging a struggle—a struggle of wits, shrewdness, cleverness—and maybe of power. How long the struggle will last, I do not know. But my beautiful Demiana must be well-guarded until it pleases God to release me."

She put her arms around his neck and said loudly, "You selfish man! You want to carry on with your struggle without giving me the satisfaction of lending a hand."

He took her two hands within his, kissing each in turn and said, "These beautiful hands must bide their time. The thorny work is for our hands only."

"No, no," she answered, "mine can do menial work too."

"My darling Demiana," he said, "you saw that I have to be at the side of my master for such long stretches. You have been here for several weeks, yet I have hardly been able to stay with you for more than a few minutes. Only today am I little free." His arms tightened around hers as he said, "I wish we could remain thus forever instead of having to be a watchdog. My time is nearly up, and these few minutes of heaven have to be foregone. But they shall be for me a fortress in my struggle."

Again she rested her head on his breast and said, "I shall be praying for you alway, more than I ever have!"

He asked, "Will you trust me and wait for me to the bitter end?"

"Bitter or sweet, I shall trust you and wait for you and ask for the blessings of the saints to be with you."

"No matter what you may hear or see?"

"I shall disbelieve my eyes and my ears and only remember how I saw you kneeling before the sanctuary today."

He took her hands and kissed them. Then taking her hand, he walked out onto the verandah where Abba Moussa was sitting and waiting for them. He sat her beside him and said, "Holy father, you have ever been my guardian angel. You were right when you advised me to tell her all. But it was worth keeping silent and getting a glimpse of heaven today." Then he turned to her and said, "And now beloved, I have to go. My time is up."

She said, "Every morning, when you are galloping away, I shall look out of the little opening in the musharabiah for as long as I am here."

He glowed as he said, "And I shall lift up my eyes to catch some of your radiance." Then kissing her and kissing the hands of Abba Moussa, he went off. Having gone a few paces, he turned and said, "One thing I want to ask of you: whenever you hear anyone talk about me, for heaven's sake don't defend me." She started to remonstrate but he put up his hand and pleaded, "Promise me!" She acquiesced with a nod. "That suffices," he answered as he turned away. Both of them watched him running down the stairs, then watched him as he jumped on Meshir's back and spurred off at top speed. He seemed to have gained more height and breadth as he sped away.

Abba Moussa seated Demiana beside him again and for sometime remained silent. Then he said most tenderly, "The blessings of our Lord and of all the saints be with both of you, and may the Loving Father graciously hasten the day of peace and security."

She put her head on his shoulder and wept quietly.

***

That very same evening, Demiana was sorely put to the test concerning her promise. Mena walked into the house with Zoheir in his wake. It was her first meeting with Zoheir since he had left Samanoud months ago. He paraded his fineries as usual and started boasting of his expenditure and of the many admirers who crossed his path. She listened to his boasting, busying herself with her fancy work as she smiled to herself. She half-expected him to start his gossip as soon as he finished showing off—and she braced herself for it.

Sure enough, the conversation began to turn from his person to his newly-made acquaintances in the court. Then he smiled maliciously and, turning to Demiana, he said, "Did you hear the latest scandal?"

She answered, "Have you no taste except for scandalous stories?"

"Oh no," he said, "I do have a taste for other things. But when rumors start around Guirguis..."

Mena interposed, "Are there no scandals but those around Guirguis? Or did you cultivate the comradeship of those courtiers you just mentioned only to know the latest of tales and adventures about Guirguis?"

Zoheir guffawed loudly as he answered, "There you have it. I did get into the court just to find out how thinly Guirguis is covering himself."

Mena asked hotly, "Very clever of you, I am sure."

Demiana kept cool. She even winked to her brother to keep silent. Then she changed the subject, asking Zoheir about his house and taunting him for never asking them to go there, if only to see his parents. This set him off once more talking of his person, and his belongings, and the number of attendants he has for his own personal requirements. But soon enough, he reverted back to the subject of Guirguis, saying with no introduction, "Surely you heard, Mena, of Guirguis being in love with Fatima, the woman-in-waiting from the Wali's harem. Poor fellow. He dared to fall in love with a woman-in-waiting, exposing his life to danger."

Mena could not keep his anger, and he said with fury, "I could cut off that poisonous tongue of yours."

This remark did not upset Zoheir; he was really upset by Demiana's silence—and even that smile on her face! So he continued with more malice, "You see, even Demiana is silent. She has nothing to say in his defense."

She still smiled and added, "Cousin Zoheir, say whatever you will. It makes no difference with me."

He asked, "How is it that you don't mind that your dear cousin is dragging himself and the family honor in the dust?"

She answered, "The Father of all mercies help him—and help us all." Her words silenced him, and after a few minutes of such silence, she broke it with innocent conversation, and things went on smoothly for the rest of the evening. Mariam also joined in shortly thereafter. She gently reproached Zoheir for not coming to see them more often, and for not taking her to see his parents. He remained for dinner.

***

Another week passed, and Demiana thought it time to

go back to Samanoud. It was midday, and as she was putting away her things, she remembered the experiences of the previous Friday. Silence was all around her; Mena had not come back, and Mariam was out on her weekly round of charity.

Suddenly, the silence was broken by hurried treading feet and an insistent knock. She ran out to see who it was, her heart beating very fast. It was Zoheir. He looked ruffled as he said, "Come Demiana, come quick. Guirguis has been stabbed by the Wali himself and is sorely wounded."

She felt dizzy at the news, but steadied herself and asked, "Where do you want me to go?"

He answered, pulling her by the hand, "Don't you want to see him before he breathes his last?"

She resisted saying, "No, no I can't go with you."

"But Guirguis is dying, and you may not reach him in time."

She was quite frightened and accepted to be dragged by him. He lifted her onto his horse, sat beside her, and galloped off to the court. She was so agitated that she had not even taken a veil. When they reached the palace gate, they dismounted, and he took her by the hand and ran in with her into the hall where the Wali and his courtiers sat. He led her right up to the divan on which the Wali reclined with Guirguis sitting next to him and said, "Here my lord is the woman I told you of, and I have brought her to you as I promised."

She stood there transfixed, while all those present stared at her. She saw that Guirguis clutched at the cross hanging on his breast, but that was the only outward sign of the tumult within his heart, for he continued his laughter and joined with the others in looking at her. Then turning to the Wali, he said in a light tone, "A comely woman indeed my lord, but these Coptic women are wildcats."

The Wali answered, "I know they are, but is there no way of taming them?"

"Well," started Guirguis. He was getting off his seat and standing beside Demiana, pretending to take a closer view at her while looking daggers at Zoheir.

"Well," reiterated the Wali, "Suppose we give her over to the custody of Fatima for a few days and see how she manages her." There were dissenting voices amid the crowd, but Guirguis managed to keep his outward coolness and laughed off their clamor.

When their voices subsided, the Wali said, "Are you to manage my own affairs? None can soothe me but Guirguis and his ever ready wit and laughter." Then smiling to his favorite, he said, "Guirguis, you lead her to Fatima."

Guirguis could not yet trust to leave the room. He turned to Zoheir and ordered him to call in Shenouti. He silently obeyed. Shenouti came in, and Guirguis said, "My lord, I can't part company with you even to obey you when there is someone else to perform your behest. We were relating a most wonderful tale when Zoheir broke in upon us, and I am aching to complete it. So kindly order Shenouti to lead the woman to Fatima."

The Wali sat up and looked for a while at Guiguis standing beside Demiana. The two of them standing side by side stirred him in an incomprehensible fashion; he even felt a little awed, and he said, "Right, Guirguis. Shenouti, you lead the woman to the apartment of Fatima."

When Shenouti led her out, she was still dazed. The whole thing passed before her eyes as though it were a nightmare. She felt strangely dizzy, and Shenouti had to put his arm around her to steady her. When they reached an open court, he seated her down, got some water from the fountain, and cooled her forehead. Then he left her for a few minutes and stood aside in silence.

She regained her composure gradually, then said brokenly, "I never thought... he could... lie... so glibly... and in such grave matters."

Shenouti came to her side and asked gently, "I suppose my lady Mariam was out when the rascal came to you?"

"Yes," she was silent again.

Shenouti left her once more to her silence, then said quietly, "If you can walk now, will you come with me? I must go back and give answer to Guirguis."

The mere mention of his name gave her strength, so she stood up firmly and said, "Lead me where you want." He led her gently through long corridors and onto arcaded verandahs, while she related to him what happened. Then finally he knocked on a beautifully carved door. When it was opened, he led her into a cool sumptuous room, seated her on a very soft divan, then stood talking in an inaudible tone to a very amiable looking elderly woman.

When he finished talking, the woman came towards her, and Shenouti said, "Lady Fatima, this is lady Demiana."

The elderly lady sat beside her and put her aching head on her shoulder saying, "Oh my dear, you are most welcome here. By the Prophet,[43] while you are here, I will guard you as the apple of my eye."

Demiana felt strangely at ease with this woman who she barely knew, and smiling at Shenouti, she said, "We will not keep you any longer."

He answered, "Now that you are in kind and safe hands, I will go. Doubtless, master Guirguis is awaiting." He bent down and kissed the hands of the two women respectfully, then disappeared, shutting the door behind him.

When Shenouti went to tell Guirguis that he had fulfilled his errand, he found that things had become normal again, but that Zoheir had disappeared.

***

For three days, Demiana stayed in the sumptuous apartment of Fatima. She was treated as a princess, and every possible thing was done to please her. She knew that she could trust Fatima, and the latter's kindness and concern was great. But in spite of all that, her heart was heavy within her. She could not help feeling that something terrible was going to happen because of her rash belief in Zoheir's lies. But how could it ever have occurred to her that things could go to such depths! She ate very little and slept very little. She mumbled to herself all day long saying, "Lord have mercy," and tried to repeat all the prayers she knew by heart in order to push away the evil thoughts that were invading her. She wondered if her parents knew of what had happened to

---

43   That is, Muhammad, the founder of Islam.

her. Thus, in spite of all the services offered to her, and the sumptuous couch accorded to her, she became very pale. Her eyes grew wider, and her beautiful black hair fell over her shoulder unbraided. She looked quite fragile.

Once a day, Shenouti came in to ask about her and comfort her fears, but she merely smiled at him weakly without saying a word.

On the third day, late in the afternoon, Fatima told her that she had to go out in order to ask about her six-year-old grandson, as word was sent that he fell and broke his arm while playing. Demiana was very sorry to hear that, and urged her to take Mena with her.

"He's already been there and did good work," said Fatima. "The boy's father called him immediately, for there is no doctor as clever as your brother." She bent over Demiana and kissed her, continuing, "I am only sorry to have to leave you. I wish you would listen to my advice and stop worrying like that. Come." She put her arm gently around Demiana to help her up, and led her to an arched window overlooking an open court with luscious growth. Then she said, "See all this beauty and look up to the blue sky. Before you have had enough time to admire it all, I shall be back."

She kissed Demiana again, who, in turn, put her arms around Fatima's neck and fondly kissed her saying, "I am sorry to be so ungrateful. The scenery is really beautiful, and I shall try to obey you."

So Fatima took leave, ordering her eunuch to sit by the door and not to open it for anyone. Demiana sat by the window and looked out. The scene eased her nerves, and the cool evening air soothed her aching forehead to the extent of making her forget her worries. Feeling relaxed after the heavy tension, she dozed off. The silence was complete.

Suddenly a loud heavy knock roused her peaceful rest. The eunuch said, "Lady Fatima is out, so whoever you are, you are not to come in now."

A severe reprimand was heard, and the poor eunuch frantically opened the door, for it was none other than the Wali in person. He came in, kicked the eunuch to close the door, and walked towards the window where Demiana sat.

She stood up like one stung and said, "Keep where you are. If you come any nearer, I will throw myself out of the window."

He stopped still and stood eyeing her closely. "You wouldn't do that to yourself!" he said, as though humoring a little child. In spite of her weakness and dizziness, she jumped lightly onto the window sill.

He stopped one more and was silent, measuring how next to behave when suddenly the door was opened wide. It was Guiguis, laughing and saying, "My lord, she is not quite ready for you. Have I not told you she is a wild cat?"

The Wali became furious. "Guirguis!" he shouted, "I am not in a mood to joke, so you'd better look out."

"But I'm coming to help you."

"Indeed, you are," the voice was sarcastic. "By the prophet, I am sick of you. If you don't get out, I'll just kill you and be done with you." With these words, he took out his dagger.

Guirguis put his back to the door to steady himself, and a thousand pictures raced through his head—but across these thousands of cinematographic pictures, the one outstanding and engulfing them all was Demiana, and how best to save her. Despite the tumult within—and the flashing work of his brain—outwardly he still laughed and said, "I bear a charmed life, don't you know that? Here I am, I shall stand perfectly still for you to aim, and you can't say that the target is small. Come, let's see if your skill can beat my charm."

He squared his shoulders and stood perfectly still as the dagger whizzed past him and struck the door. The tenseness that followed was broken by the voice of Guirguis: "My lord haven't I told you?"

The Wali bit his lips, remained silent for a while, then burst out, "A curse on that charm of yours!"

Guirguis eyed the Wali in silence for a while, then walked up quietly to him, put his arm around his shoulder, and said in a most soothing voice, "My lord, I am sorry, but you have worked yourself up and refused to listen to me. Look at what you were about to do. The lady here was going to throw herself out of the window, your dagger was going to send me off to the next world, and all this in the sanctuary of Lady Fatima in her absence. Three wrongs in one short moment of anger!"

The Wali passed his hand on his forehead for a few seconds, as though exorcising some demon, then said, "By the prophet, you must be a sorcerer, Guirguis. Just now I was furious against you, and would have killed you but for the charm you bear. And now I find you are right."

"Now that's the Wali I know, the friend of Guirguis. Listen to me my lord: this lady is here in safe hands, why should you be overhasty? Wait but a little, and she'll be summoning you to her side." He left the Wali, walked to

Demiana, carried her gently from off her perch, and put her very tenderly on the divan. Then he went back to the Wali saying, "Why, she's as stiff as a block of marble! Come, my lord, let's leave her until she is ready to welcome our presence."

The Wali took one look at Demiana—indeed, she was so white and motionless, she might easily have been a marble statue. Then putting his arm into that of Guirguis, he said, "You are right, my friend," and they both walked out.

When they reached the door, Guirguis pulled out the stuck dagger and handed it over to the Wali saying, "This is yours, my lord, to remind you that you should not let your anger cause you to forget your friendship."

The Wali took it, and put it back in his belt saying, "Well said, my good servant."

Demiana lay where Guirguis put her. She was quite dazed. She neither saw nor heard anything. She could only see Guirguis standing by the door, and the dagger whizzing past him. When Fatima returned, she seemed to Demiana like a shadow moving among other shadows—even her words came as an incomprehensible murmur. How many hours passed in that manner, she did not know, nor did she care to know.

She was abruptly pulled out of her lethargy by Shenouti coming in and saying in low, quick and commanding tones, "Get up and put these clothes on, for there is no time to waste." She got up as an automat, and was led by Fatima into a small room where both of them changed into the men's clothing brought by Shenouti. This fact woke Demiana up fully. She went out with Fatima and Shenouti, passed through a long subterranean corridor which seemed interminable, and finally found herself in the open. The evening shadows were already fallen, but in the semi-darkness, she could see the outline of Guirguis holding Meshir and two other horses. At the sight of him, all the tenseness of her nerves gave way, and she ran into his open arms, rested her head against his breast, and began to weep in silence. As he enveloped her within his arms, she sobbed out, "Are you alright, my beloved?"

He laughed gently as he answered, "Of course I am. Can't you see that I am?"

She stammered, "I was so frightened, and you were so admirable."

He patted her under the cheek, remarking, "See how clear the sky is, my love? In an hour, you shall be in security."

"What about you?" she asked.

His answer was confident, "Didn't you hear me telling the Wali that I bear a charmed life?" He raised her face up to him and whispered, "You are going to my dear guardian angel Abba Moussa, and you shall stay there until word comes to you."

She put up her arms around his neck and said, "I shall be thinking of you and praying for you.. and worrying over you."

He said, "Think and pray, but leave off worrying." Then, again kissing her, he lifted her up, placed her on Meshir's back, patted his neck and said, "Meshir, I never entrusted you with so precious a person before, but you are a trusted friend, so godspeed." Meshir started off like a shot, followed by the two other horses on which Fatima and Shenouti had already mounted. Guirguis shouted after them, "Be very quick Shenouti! Do not slacken your pace till you reach the haven safely!"

Shenouti obeyed implicitly; he needed not be told of the danger, and his love for Guirguis knew no bounds. An hour later, they were crossing the garden gate of the Mansion.

Abba Moussa had just bidden some guests good-bye and was about to have his dinner, when the three travelers walked into his presence in utter silence. Accustomed to surprises, he welcomed them most tenderly, adding, "You have come at a very good time. I thought I shall have dinner alone; instead, I shall enjoy your companionship." They sat down, still silent. Abba Moussa talked about diverse matters to dispel their anxiety.

When dinner was over, the two women retired, while Shenouti related to the bishop the whole episode. He listened in silent meditation. When he heard the whole story, he said, quietly, "My son, go now and rest immediately, because you have to return by dawn." Shenouti obeyed, and the man of God went to church, where he spent a whole hour travailing in silent imploring.

Chapter Three

A Mighty Travail

Very strict orders were given in the Coptic quarter that no one was to venture far beyond the gates unless absolutely necessary, and that they were to be alert and on guard. The gatekeepers were to keep the gates shut and not to open anything except the little side door to let out or let in one person at a time. They were also to be ready for emergency.

Demiana had been sent to Wissim with Fatima on the dawn of Tuesday. Tuesday passed in safety, and so did Wednesday. That evening, the Wali sent a messenger to ask about Fatima and was quite taken by surprise when he was told that the apartment was empty.

Guirguis had already gone home and was reclining lazily on a couch, reading a letter which had been sent that morning from Youannis. Mariam was sitting nearby, listening to what he had to say every now and then. She always felt happy to have Guirguis near her and to hear him talk, at times like a little child, and at others like a responsible man. She often told him that at times he reminded her very much of Big Brother, and he would smile quietly and say, "I am always striving to be like him, and it satisfies me beyond measure to be likened to him." Just now, he again reminded her of his brother—so serious was he—and she told him how proud she was of him saying, "The blessings of all the saints be with you."

She had barely finished her sentence, when Shenouti walked in looking quite upset and saying, "Master Guirguis, a messenger is here for you... from the Wali."

Guirguis got up, dressed, and came back to Mariam where she sat. He said, "I suppose he found out that the women are not there." Then bending down over her hand to kiss it, he said, "Sister Mariam, your serenity in the face of all of life's troubles has been a rock for me to lean on. I know not what may come, but I do know that whatever may happen, you will still stand firm. Give me your blessing before I go."

She put her other hand around his neck and kissed his head, saying in a steady, though very low voice, "The Blessed Saint Mary be with you, my boy." He kissed her hand again and went out, followed by Shenouti, as usual.

***

Like a caged beast, the Wali was pacing up and down his own bedroom, muttering away without waiting for an answer. There were only two men with him in his room: Hassan, Fatima's son-in-law, and Sourour, his Nubian bodyguard.

When Guirguis appeared, the Wali stopped short and shouted, "Where have the women gone?"

Guirguis feigned surprise, "Women, which women?"

"I suppose you are going to pretend that you know nothing. Well, it is Fatima and that Coptic houri I am talking of. They are not here!"

"Great God in heaven, but how comes it?"

"How comes it? You liar! you rascal! You accursed dog..." a whole volley of words continued and fell on the ears of Guirguis, while he waited in silence.

When the Wali had finished, Guirguis said, "You surprise me, my lord, talking to me like that. Why am I the one you suspect?"

"Why? Because you barred my way on Monday evening."

Guirguis laughed outright saying, "An excellent reason, my lord."

The Wali threw himself on a divan, then looking at Guirguis he said, "You have duped me, putting me off in order to smuggle her. But I shall punish you most mercilessly if you don't tell me where she is."

Guirguis walked up to the Wali's divan, sat down beside him, and reclining on one elbow he said, "Great God in heaven. Fancy my lord that you threaten me thus when you have no proof of my guilt."

The Wali asked, "Well, who then is responsible for this escape?"

"How am I to know? I haven't been there since I was

with you."

The Wali sat up and said, "You can't suspect anybody else because you know that you are the one." Again Guirguis laughed, and the Wali shouted, "You are exasperating me!" Then, staring at him for a little, he continued, "I'll kill you if you did it. Here you are next to me, and all I have to do is dig that dagger into your breast."

Guirguis remained unruffled. "Go on," he said.

Here, Hassan interposed, "My lord, surely no woman is worth that much. What is one more woman, or one less? You have so many of them, but you won't find a man like Guirguis everyday. By the Prophet, my lord, no woman deserves that much."

The Wali was somewhat at a loss. He was silent for a while, his hand playing with the edge of the dagger at his belt. Taking out the dagger, he looked at it intently for a few minutes, then mumbled, "You should not let your anger make you forget your friendship." He then put the dagger back into its place and said, "Hassan is right. It would be a shame to waste a man's life for a woman. But I must punish you, for I think no one else is to blame." He was silent again, stroked his beard, then said, "I know what I'll do with you. I'll make you an example to all the honey-tongued and smooth-smiling people. When the sun is high up tomorrow morning, I'll have you lashed forty whips minus one in the public square—unless of course, you either tell me where they are, or who the culprit is."

Hassan tried to put in a word this time also, but the Wali said, "Hold your tongue. If you continue to defend him, I'll have you punished too." At that, Hassan refrained from speaking.

Guirguis sat up. His smile disappeared, and he looked very grave. He was lost in thought, and the Wali watched him a little uneasily, for he had never seen him in such a mood. Presently, he said in quiet, measured tones, "My lord, it would not be very wise to rouse my people's indignation."

The Wali turned on him sourly, "You threaten me, you accursed dog! I'll have you lashed, and we'll see what your accursed people will do. Sourour, seize him and bind him!"

Sourour came forward, but Guirguis put his hand up and said in the same weighty manner, "No need, Sourour. I shall not run away, nor shall I ever resist. Here I am."

Sourour stopped short and looked at his master. The Wali said, "Well, Sourour, leave him." Sourour stepped back. Guirguis leaned against the cushions on the divan, crossed his hands on his breast, and transformed into his trance-like attitude.

The Wali, looking at him, felt the same awe he always felt before Guirguis when he had that other-worldly look. He got up briskly from his place and shook him as though trying to exorcise him and shouted "Get out of this room, Guirguis!" Guirguis made no sign of hearing, and the Wali came towards him and shouted again the same order.

Guirguis said, half-dreamily, "Were you speaking to me, my lord?"

"Yes I was, and I was telling you to leave this room!"

"Can you trust me out of your sight?"

"Yes, I can. You said you wouldn't resist, and I trust your word."

Guirguis smiled cynically and said, It's very strange that

you can trust an accursed dog."

The Wali got annoyed. "Get out, I said! And don't speak anymore."

"Where shall I go?"

"Into the guest room assigned to you until I send for you."

Guirguis stood up, and resuming his usual lightness, he said, "Good night, my lord. And pleasant dreams." Then he walked out.

Shenouti was waiting for him outside and followed him. When they got into their assigned room, Guirguis sat in bed and told Shenouti all that happened. Then stretching himself on the bed, he went off to sleep. Shenouti kept vigil and prayed until the rays of the sun woke Guirguis up.

***

There was no little commotion in the town. The news spread like wild fire, and Guirguis was not a man with whom anyone could be indifferent; people either loved or hated him. Thus the streets became crowded, and there was shouting and dissension. The patriarch, upon hearing of what was to be dealt to Guirguis, went over in haste to the palace. The whole group of courtiers were present. Even among them there was dissension, for there were those who thought that even an 'accursed infidel' should not be dealt with in this fashion, as he was no common man. Others clamored loudly that due to his high position, it was better to punish him thus and make him lose his dignity before all people. But whether in favor of Guirguis or against him, pleas and threats only made the Wali more obstinate.

Just a little before noon, Guirguis strode out in the midst of the big crowd to the public square to be lashed. The only ones who were permitted to follow him were Mena and Shenouti. He rode Meshir, in an easy trot—head high with a smile on his face. He even greeted his acquaintances as he passed. When he came to the public place, he dismounted and bared his own body. Then, crossing his hands on his breast, he ordered Sourour to start the lashing in a voice which everyone heard. Those who came to jeer were dumbfounded, and those who were sympathetic and indignant swelled with pride because of the calm of Guirguis who stood unshaken. He had that faraway look in his eyes as the lashes fell on his back; not even a groan escaped his lips. For the onlookers, it may well have been Mena who was beaten, for his face was crimson, his eyes were blazing, and he bit his lips.

Halfway through, the Wali rode into the square with a group of his courtiers. The gracious way Guirguis took the beating infuriated him. He shouted, "Sourour, you are not doing your job properly! You are lax. Come, release all your strength on him!" In spite of the doubled efforts of the Nubian giant, Guirguis remained unmoved. The Wali muttered a few curses and walked away in haste, for he sensed the swelling anger in the crowd.

When the thirty-nine lashes were dealt, Sourour walked off, and Mena came to the rescue. The tensity of the nerves having given way, the people crowded on Guirguis as he was laid face downwards on a heap of caftans offered by several onlookers. When Mena had washed the wounds and dressed them with soothing ointment, Shenouti, aided by friends, carried Guirguis home.

***

Mariam was waiting for him at the top of the stairs. Since he left her the night before, she had gone to the icon of the blessed Virgin, knelt down, and wept bitterly. She was unable to stop the flow of her tears. A few minutes later, however, she reminded herself that it was no time for weeping, for she must do all she could to help Guirguis. Didn't St. John Kame[44] say, "If you fall into temptation, ask not God to take it away from you, but ask Him to give you the strength to bear it?" Guirguis was to be sorely tried, and her love for him constrained her to pray for him. She had repeated, "Lord have mercy" all night long, and the Lord did have mercy, for the Wali could have just stabbed him there and then. And now, she willed to rush to church to have the priest offer a special liturgy on his behalf. Within a few minutes, she was going down the stairs and off to church. She headed straight for the Lady's church of *Al-Muallakah,* and at the gate she met the priest. He, too, had heard of what was happening to Guirguis and was walking in to church to do the Liturgy on his behalf of his own accord. When he saw Mariam, he greeted her in silence, and they both walked into the church. Many people joined them, and

---

44 St. John Kame (or Kama) is a saintly father. Famous for living with his wife as brother and sister, he later went to the monastery of St. Macarius to become a monk. There, he was famous for teaching 300 brethren the Midnight Praises, such that the Virgin Mary appeared to him and commanded that his dwelling be a church named after her. His feast day is Kiahk 25, or January 3.

St. John Kame

after the service, a special song of praise was offered to the Blessed Virgin. Then the congregation went out—all except Mariam, who remained behind.

When she was all alone, she went and knelt beside the iconostasis, and besought the Father of all mercies to send His angel to strengthen Guirguis. She remained within the church until she heard the watchman outside declaring that it was midday, then she quietly slipped out of the church and went home. Arriving there, she went straight to the Virgin's icon, knelt before it, and continued her prayers. Only when she heard the sound of footsteps at the front gate did she rise and run to the door.

She greeted Guirguis with her usual gentle smile, put a hand on his head, and walked beside him to his room. When he was put in his bed and everyone left, she sat down beside him in silence, passing her hand on his forehead and through his hair gently and soothingly as she always did when he was upset or in pain.

Both of them were silent for a while, then Guirguis said with a smile, "It is amazing, I cannot really describe to you the power that was given me. The Lord of all comfort sent His angel to strengthen me, and the angel overshadowed me with his wings. As I stood there with my hands crossed over my breast, Big Brother stood before me with you on his right and Demiana on his left. Truly, I can never describe the inward serenity that filled my whole being as I found myself under the wings of God's angel and with such loving company."

Mariam listened to him while her whole face lit up. She laid her hand on his head, then said, "If you had seen the number of people who flocked to church to pray for you,

you would not be amazed that such strength was given you. You see, I went there early this morning to ask the priest to offer the Liturgy on your behalf, but I met him at the church door going in of his own accord to pray for you. Soon, many people came—all of them without being told, for I had no time to send word to anyone. Surely, Big Brother was praying for you with the company of "the just men made perfect."[45] Her voice vibrated with the joy she felt within her heart.

Guirguis said, "It is really most comforting to know that there are so many loving hearts praying to the Father on one's behalf."

"Yes," answered Mariam. "This is the invisible link that upholds and sustains us all through the strain and stress of this world." They were silent for a few seconds, then Mariam said, "Now you must go to sleep." She got up, prepared for him a hot drink made of some sweet-smelling herb, and gave it to him spoon by spoon saying, "The most merciful Father who gave you strength to stand so bravely will also give you restful sleep." When he drank what she had prepared for him, she chanted for him in a low sweet voice as though he were a little child. Then he fell asleep.

She sat watching him for some time while tears of joy flowed down her cheeks, and her lips repeated, "Thank you, my God." Then she tiptoed out of the room.

***

---

45 Heb. 12:23

Riots broke throughout Al-Fustat[46], just as Guirguis had forewarned the Wali. For two whole weeks, the city was in turmoil—street skirmishes and brawls became a common sight. To make matters worse, the Wali gave orders to kill and pillage—as a sort of defiance—just to see how it would work to squash the dissent. Many people were killed and whole quarters were set aflame, so much so that the Wali himself became alarmed at the mischief he had set afoot. He had to establish order at the sword's point. Thus, after the mob had rioted and killed, they in turn were killed by the Wali's troops.

During those terrible days, the strict orders which Guirguis had the foresight to give beforehand were rigidly carried out, so that the victims among the Copts were minimal.

He, himself, lay in bed while his wounds healed. Mena watched over him with great devotion. He never tired of recounting how simply marvelous Guirguis was, and how proud he and Shenouti felt in spite of their agony. Every little detail of the whole incident was recounted with loving accents. When Mariam heard the whole story from Mena for the first time, she smiled and said, "Does not the Psalmist say, 'The Lord is strength in time of trouble?'"[47]

Strange as it seemed, Guirguis became stronger and handsomer. After the first few days, the pain had completely subsided. The devotion of Mena was unsurpassable, and Mariam's care was ceaseless. She seemed to feel no fatigue in the service of Guirguis, who remonstrated with her several times, to no avail, that she should give herself a little rest.

---

46   Part of Old Cairo.

47   Psalm 37:39

She would only smile benignantly and say, "Your service is my rest." Thus with Mena's devotion and Mariam's care—and his own feeling of well-being and peaceful living among those who really loved him—he recuperated rapidly and was soon better than his old self.

The fury of the city subsided two weeks after Guirguis had been lashed. He was more than well by that time. Still, he lingered a third week within the sanctuary of his own home. Then, one Friday noon, he sauntered forth to the Wali's palace. He rode Meshir at a leisurely pace, and his reappearance on the streets of Al-Fustat stirred the city. His friends greeted him joyfully, and he had to stop Meshir several times in order to shake hands with those who eagerly came up to him. His foes felt an inward pang of jealousy; it was incomprehensible how that "accursed infidel" rode forth in the city as if he were a hero!

And hero he was! For all well-remembered his stand. Now he seemed to have grown taller and broader. They tried to humiliate him, and instead he became more exalted in the eyes of the people.

He had timed his ride so that he would reach the gate of the palace just as the Wali was coming back from his Friday prayers. By the time the Wali and his entourage did arrive, Guirguis was waiting beside the gate. He did not dismount, but lifted his hand to his forehead in the usual greeting and said, "*Salaam*, my lord."

The Wali stood still, somewhat taken by surprise. Then, regaining himself, he said, "What? Is that you, Guirguis?"

"Yes, my lord."

"But you are in very good health, and all smiles."

"Allah be praised, my lord. He gave me this superb health. So why should I not smile, when God has so mercifully favored me?"

"Favored you indeed! Sourour beats you like he has never beat anyone in his life, and we thought he could beat you to within a few inches of your life, and what is the result?"

Guirguis laughed outright. "How can a human being undo what the Almighty does?" Seeing the Wali's color change, he added with a triumphant note that annoyed all his antagonists, "Did I not tell you that I bear a charmed life? Isn't it time you realized this truth?"

All were silent at this remark as the Wali and his courtiers eyed Guirguis and his men. Then regaining his old ways, Guiguis said sportingly, "Hail, my lord! Is that the welcome you accord an old and trusted friend?" His laughing voice broke the tension, and he dismounted with his usual agility and came rapidly to the Wali, holding the reins of his horse and saying, "Let me help you to dismount, my lord, just as was my wont to do. You used to say that you did not like anyone to help you come off your horse but me." The Wali acquiesced, and presently, the two men walked into the sumptuous gardens, while the others followed just in the same old way. Several courtiers shrugged their shoulders, and more than one look was exchanged between them as they walked behind Guirguis, who once more towered over them all and filled them with an impalpable sense of fear.

Three weeks passed, during which Guirguis resumed his life as though nothing had happened. Once more, he took his seat on the Wali's divan, and once more, the Wali listened to his jokes. Political matters were growing tense, for rumors and skirmishes were daily happening, and the Caliph Marwan[48] was preparing to fight the rebel leaders who claimed to have more right to the caliphate. These rumors made the populace more unruly, and emboldened some of the courtiers even to the point of rudeness. Thus the atmosphere of the court became more and more tense. Yet in spite of all the tension, Guirguis managed to keep his equanimity, and he was still able to relate tales in his inimitable fashion. He still was able to say jokes that set the Wali roaring, and made him forget for a while the worries of the state. That power of Guirguis to keep cool infuriated his antagonists all the more, and not a day passed without a few malicious remarks being made, which were aimed at rousing the Wali against him. But Guirguis had become so accustomed to their venom, that he just shrugged his shoulders at them.

Once, the malice was a little too sharp and angered the Wali against the tongue who said it. Guirguis, smiling confidently—and somewhat condescendingly—said in his most suave voice, "My lord, anger not yourself because of a little remark. Your health is too precious, and these pinpricks who aim at me cannot reach me." And he continued to tell the Wali a few more of his anecdotes. Later on, as he walked out with the Wali to lunch, he turned to the malicious courtier and said, "You seem to have forgotten, my friend, that I bear a charmed life."

***

---

48   Marwan II of Umayyad (reigned from 744-750) was the ruthless Muslim leader, who ruled over the Middle East at the time.

Another week passed, and it was again Friday. The Wali parted company with Guirguis as the whole train of courtiers went out to the mosque at the hour of prayer. The Wali was in a tense mood; the news from the Caliph were not very reassuring. Moreover, a few malicious remarks about "the infidel" who always parted company with them at the gate of the mosque made the Wali frown but remain silent.

Guirguis galloped to *Al-Muallakah* church as usual. His prayers were more fervent than ever, and as he walked out, he lifted up his eyes towards the *mushrabiah* and sighed, wishing that Demiana was here to soothe his aching heart and infuse him with new strength for the struggle he had to wage continuously. He then bowed his head for a few seconds, murmuring to himself, "How long, my God, how long?" Then somehow—he did not know how—new strength was fused into him. He lifted up his head and walked briskly back to the iconostasis of the church, crossed himself, and said almost in a rapture: "The Lord hear thee in the day of trouble, and send you help from His sanctuary.[49] Thank you, my God, thank you, for verily, You are a present help in time of need." Then, repeating the Lord's prayer, he committed himself to the care of the Blessed Virgin and the saints, and walked out repeating Paul's words, "Whether we live or whether we die, we are the Lord's."[50]

On his way back, he met a few young men who were among his ardent enthusiasts, and they followed him, talking in a light mood. At the gate of the palace, Guirguis and his group encountered the Wali and his train. Greetings

---

49 Psalm 20:1, 2.

50 Rom. 14:18.

were interchanged, and all of them walked into the palace. It being Friday and lunchtime, people were allowed to walk in and share of the Wali's bounty. But the Wali was still a little morose, and Guirguis sensed it from his silence. The new strength which filled him as he left the church overflowed him now and made him seem to the rival courtiers as though he was standing on a higher plane. He talked and laughed, and his whole being expanded like a rose. Ease and inner poise seemed to emanate from him, and it filled them with deeper sense of incomprehensible awe. That feeling, coupled with the silence of the Wali, made them talk in hushed voices. Only Guirguis and his young men were hilarious.

Their jollity suddenly roused the Wali, who said, "Who dares abuse our bounty with such unbecoming hilarity when matters of state call for soberness?"

Several voices answered at once, "The young men who came in with Guirguis."

One of the courtiers said, laughing maliciously, "Since the famous incident, Guirguis finds the company of young men more befitting that that of women."

Before Guirguis was aware of what he was doing, he slapped the speaker on the mouth with the back of his palm, and his eyes burned like live coals as he surveyed the whole group of courtiers.

There was a hush for a few seconds, then the voice of the Wali broke in, "To prison with Guirguis and his whole group."

The young men started and were about to remonstrate, when Guirguis said very lightly, "Come along, friends. Prison can possibly be more congenial than such deceitful company." And they all walked out, surrounded by guards.

***

Mena was not present during this unexpected incident. When Shenouti came home to give the news, Mena's usual anger rose to its highest pitch, and for several days, Mariam kept him inside the house, not even letting him out of her sight for fear that he might go out and commit some folly. He ate very little and slept very little. He spent most of his time pacing up and down his room or in the balcony on which Mariam sat, like some caged wild animal. Gradually, Mariam's soothing presence and calm confidence invaded his soul, and he found himself regaining his appetite and his sleep. Then, as she saw him becoming more himself, she would recount to him the most exciting tales of Guirguis's adventures. Her influence made him laugh at his own folly for getting into such a fit.

Twelve days passed. Mena, though he had become quite normal, refused to go to the court. He told Mariam, "I don't want to see the face of that man. Had you not restrained me, I would have rushed out on that first day and killed him. Now, I don't want to set eyes on him."

Mariam looked at him very benignantly and said in her quiet and sweet way, "My dear Mena, your life is not yours to throw it away in this rash manner. You are both a renowned physician and surgeon. You must bide your time. Do you remember how impetuous Guirguis was as a lad? Look at him now."

Mena's face brightened, "I must confess, I stand amazed

at the mastery Guirguis has acquired over himself. I shall never forget, in this world or the world to come, how he stood while the lashes fell on his back."

Here his speech was broken by Shenouti, who walked in and said with no introduction, "Dr Mena, you are urgently wanted at the court."

"Now? At this hour? It's dinnertime. What for?"

"A messenger has just arrived to say that the Wali was seized by a fit of fever. He is even delirious."

Mena got up as the physician in him was roused. Mariam stood up, too. She walked up to him and put her hands on his shoulders, and said in a voice full of confident assurance, "God be with you, my son, and the blessings of our Lady. This is indeed your hour. Strive with the fever, not only for the Wali's life, but for the safety of all our loved ones."

He took her two hands in his and said, "The Lord help me, but I must tell you before I go that your courage is an example to us, and your calm confidence inspires us all. Pray for me." He bent and kissed each hand in turn. Then he walked out.

***

The Wali was indeed delirious. He was raving like a madman, and the name of Guirguis was often repeated by him.

For twenty more hours, Mena contended with the fever. At last he succeeded. The Wali came to himself, recognized Mena, and then fell into a deep restful sleep. Mena watched by his side until he woke up refreshed, though weak.

Mena smiled at him and asked in a concerned voice, "How are you feeling now, my lord?"

The pale man answered weakly, "I am much better, thanks be to Allah." Mena prepared a drink and offered it to him. He drank it avidly, then said quietly, "Why have I not seen you at the court lately?"

Mena smiled faintly, "I was not feeling very well, my lord."

"What! Even you, Mena, get unwell like the rest of us! How come?"

Mena said firmly, "The imprisonment of Guirguis upset me so much that I became unwell."

The Wali frowned and was silent for a while, then said, "That cousin of yours baffles my comprehension. I love him at times, and hate him at others. His company is indispensable to me, and yet I order him to be lashed and imprisoned. At times, he is my closest friend. At others I cannot forget that he is an infidel!" Here, the Wali fell silent once more while Mena held his wrist counting his pulse.

Silence followed for a few minutes, then Mena said, "Just now, you seem to forget that I, too, am an infidel."

The Wali turned a little pale and said, "By the Prophet, I forgot that."

Mena left the wrist of the Wali and said, "But I do not forget that now you are my patient. I do not like to boast, but maybe it would be right to tell you that since I was called to your side on Tuesday evening, I have watched by your side contending with the fever with all the skill I possess."

Another pause of silence followed, then the Wali said, "Maybe you have thus struggled for fear that my men might kill you if I die."

Mena could not help himself from laughing a long hearty laugh, then said, "My lord, will you permit me to be frank?" The Wali nodded his assent, and Mena continued, "Rebellions are everywhere. The populace here are unruly, and your courtiers are divided against themselves into several camps, as you well know. Pray, who among your men would really care to kill me when you are gone?" He got up from his chair and sat on the edge of the Wali's bed looking at him seriously, then said in slow measured tones, "No my lord, I did all I could to save your life for two reasons: the first is that, as a physician, I feel triumphant when my patient becomes well; the second is that when I succeed in saving your life, I shall ask in return the release of Guirguis and all those imprisoned with him, whether they be Copts or Muslims."

"Indeed!" said the Wali. After a pause of a few seconds, he asked, "And what if I refuse your request?"

Mena got up and walked to the window and back, then said, "I shall try very hard not to forget that I am your physician!" Then suddenly, his eyes darted to the dagger which the Wali had aimed at Guirguis. He walked briskly towards it, gave it to the Wali and asked, "Do you remember what Guirguis told you when he gave you back that dagger?" The Wali closed his eyes. Mena continued, "Anyhow, you must have some more sleep now, you are still a little weak. This conversation may fatigue you."

The Wali said imploringly, "Please, don't leave me."

Mena put a gentle hand on his shoulder and said, "I

shall not leave you, but what about Guirguis? Even while you raved, his name was on your lips."

"He haunts me ... he haunts me. What can I do with him?"

"Release him. I am sure his tales and his jokes will speed your recovery."

"I cannot. I fear him."

"Have no fear, don't you know how he strives to please you?"

"Well, I am the Wali. I have the power of life and death over him."

"No you don't. If you had, you would have long ago killed him. Anyways, now I have the power of life over you."

"Life... life... not death. You said life."

"Yes. I deliberately refused to say death, because I am no traitor."

"Then please give me that drink you gave me just before I slept so comfortably."

"I shall prepare it. Meanwhile..."

The Wali interrupted, "Call Hassan for me."

Mena, still pounding at his medicine herb, walked to the door and called Hassan. When the latter arrived, the Wali said, "Go and release Guirguis and all who were imprisoned with him. I think we were overhasty that day."

"Allah give my lord long life," said Hassan.

He was about to leave when the Wali said, "Tell Guirguis to come straight here. By the Prophet, I miss his tales."

Mena prepared the medicine and was about to give it to the Wali when Hassan reappeared with Guirguis, who looked as jovial as ever. He said, "Peace be unto you, my lord. I was sorry to hear you were in bed and therefore came with Hassan in great haste to see you. I hope, by Allah's mercy, that now you are better."

Mena gave the Wali the drink and answered in his stead, "He is certainly much better, but now that you have come to entertain him with all your amusing stories stories and jokes, he shall be well in no time."

The Wali drank, then said, "Guirguis, that cousin of yours is most persistent. He contended with the fever insistently, and then he contended with me for your release just as much."

Guirguis laughed saying, "My lord, if it pleases you not to release me, I will go back to prison."

The Wali caught his hand, "No, no don't go. You know Guirguis, your mere presence has given me strength. It is amazingly incomprehensible."

Guirguis sat on the edge of the Wali's bed and looked at him quietly. Smiling, he said, "You see my lord, the charm I bear has an infectious effect. Those who are my friends receive of my strength."

The Wali put up his hand, "Please don't talk like that, you make me afraid."

Guirguis played with the cross on his breast for a while, then said, "What are your orders, Dr. Mena, for I see no one else in the room?"

Mena answered, "My lord should go to sleep now. He is well on his way to recovery. In a day or two, he shall be up and about, by the will of Allah. Then you can entertain him with your tales."

Guirguis asked, "Can I stay until my lord sleeps? I have just a tale or two which happened to me in prison, and I am quite eager to relate them because they are most amusing."

The Wali pleaded, "Do say them, your pleasant voice is a tonic."

Guirguis looked at Mena and said, "Do you hear that, Dr. Mena? Maybe my tales will work in conjunction with your medicine."

Mena answered, "I actually just told him that before you came in."

"Yes," said the Wali, "Do speak."

Guirguis spoke. The Wali was so delighted, that he forgot his ailment.

A whole hour passed, then Mena said, "Don't you think you should go to sleep for a while now, my lord?"

"Alright, have it your way, Mena. But by the Prophet, your cousin is a magician."

Guirguis got up. "By your leave, my lord, I would like to go home for a while. I shall surely be back before you wake up."

The Wali said, "If you promise not to be too late, I will give you leave."

Mena was about to speak, but Guirguis did not give him time. He said, "Of course, I will not be late."

With that, he left.

***

One beautiful May evening, Guirguis was returning home from the Wali's palace. He was going at an easy pace, oblivious of the world around him. Meshir seemed to sense his master's dreaminess and ambled noiselessly along. It was quite out of the ordinary that Guirguis should be returning home at this early hour, but a messenger had arrived earlier in the day summoning the Wali to meet the Caliph's envoy at Al-Quosier.[51] The Wali left the city in great haste, giving his courtiers three days leave. When they had all bidden him godspeed, each went his way. Guirguis patted Meshir gently on the neck saying, "Well, my trusty friend, we have three days of freedom. What say you about going to Wissim?"

Shenouti, riding alongside, said exaltedly, "This would be most welcome."

Guirguis laughed heartedly saying, "I did not ask you, Shenouti, my friend. In fact, I shall probably leave you behind."

Shenouti felt a little disconcerted, then regaining his elation he said, "I have always followed you through your darkest hour, even unto the brightest. I shall not let you go alone—unless of course, stern duty bid me stay."

"That's just it, my dearest companion. Your stay here may be quite necessary. Now, run ahead and tell Lady Mariam of our unexpected short respite, while I turn aside for a few minutes to give thanks to God."

Shenouti trotted off. Guirguis, having said his evening

---

51 City in Eastern Egypt, by the coast of the Red Sea.

prayers, rode peaceably on; both horse and rider felt an inward contentment. The passers-by gazed Guirguis in awe. He had that faraway look that always made them feel that he was in touch with the Invisible—and none dared so much as to greet him.

Arriving home, he found Mariam waiting for him quite radiant, saying "I have already packed what you need for your journey." Guirguis kissed her hands joyously, then asked about Mena. Mariam said that he was still out, and asked if he was to go along to Wissim.

Guiguis said, "If he cares to go, then well and good."

They sat in the inner court while the fountains splashed, talking very little. They had been there for half an hour, when Mena ran in saying, "Guirguis, Youannis has turned up and is actually coming up the doorsteps."

Guirguis sprang to his feet, "Youannis in person! Some very important matter must have brought him."

"Indeed," said Youannis, as he walked into the room. Guirguis went forward to meet him, and both men embraced each other heartily.

Guirguis then asked, "What guided your footsteps hither?"

Youannis said, "I have come to meet the Wali"

"But he is not here. Had he been here, you would not have found me at home."

"Not here! But where is he? You see, I am not the only one coming to meet him. Several leaders of our people have agreed to come together, thinking that our number may be good enough reason for him to change his policy."[52]

"The Lord have mercy on us. But dear Youannis, did you not get word that the Wali is most ill-tempered these days? You see, some people came to him a short while ago telling him of the rise of a new faction in the far end of the Caliphate who think there is a nearer heir to the Muslim Prophet than the present Prince of the Faithful, and is therefore the more rightful ruler.[53] This afternoon, a messenger summoned the Wali to El Quossier to meet the special envoy of the Caliph. They are probably meeting to plan how to appease this faction."

"What shall we then do? Idle quietly here at Al-Fustat until he comes back?"

"Nay, I have a better plan. I am going to Wissim. Why not come along—all of you? I have always found the solution to my problems with our most venerable Abba Moussa."

"Excellent, we'll all go. I'd better go to the Patriarchate to see who are the ones who came, and tell them of your proposal without delay."

Mariam remonstrated, saying that he didn't rest or have any refreshments since he came in, and that Mena had better go instead.

Youannis was about to refuse her request when Mena jumped up saying, "I shall run in haste—and I suppose you can trust me, dearest brother." The next moment, he disappeared and his hasty footsteps were heard on the stairs as he ran away.

---

52 Meaning the increasing taxes, or jizya, imposed on the Coptic Christians.

53 The faction mentioned was likely the Abbasids.

Mariam led the two men into the living room where she seated them in a cool recess and brought them some refreshments. She then sat down and joined in their conversation as they discussed the state of affairs.

In less than half an hour, Mena came back telling them that all the men expected had arrived, and that they unanimously assented to go to Wissim.

Youannis then got up saying, "I think it is only fitting that I go to meet them and plan with them when to go and how."

Guirguis said, "Very well, I'll come along with you."

Mariam added, "Do ask them to honor us by coming to stay with us here. It is only fair to ask them. What say you Guirguis? Hasn't the house of Big Brother been a house open to all for years and years?" Guirguis assented. He kissed her hands quietly and so did Youannis, then both went out with Shenouti following close at their heels.

They came back for dinner, bringing with them some men from the group. After dinner, they sat out in the open court, talking quietly until midnight.

Mariam said, "I really don't want to annoy you, but don't you all think that it would be wiser to go to sleep now and get refreshed? You have to wake up by sunrise and start on your journey." They all assented.

Next morning at sunrise, they started for Wissim. They looked for Guirguis, but he was nowhere to be found.

Youannis smiled quietly as he said, "He is already at Wissim. He started on his journey at midnight when we all went to sleep. Of course you all know the tie that binds him to Abba Moussa."

One of the men from the group added amiably, "We also know of the tie that binds him to the fair Demiana, and we have heard, with pride, of his stand when he was lashed. We all hope to attend their wedding very soon."

Long before the first rays of the sun shot through the eastern sky, Meshir and Guirguis were ambling leisurely towards the gate of the Mansion in Wissim. It was during the second half of the lunar month, and Guirguis found that the moonlight was sufficient for his journey. Giving his injunctions to Shenouti, who was to stay behind and keep an eye on things in general, he got into his private boat—he and Meshir alone. The boatman set the sails and left the breeze to do its job, as they wished to arrive after dawn. Horse and rider slept in the back of the boat.

On arriving, the boatman woke them up. Guirguis jumped to the shore, followed by Meshir. He stood for a few short minutes, scanning the wide expanse stretching before him. His memory whirled back to the first visit paid to that dear old man who has meant so much in his life. Then memory flitted to his first meeting with Demiana and her brothers, and the bond of fellowship that made them one. For a few short minutes, it was not the wide expanse of earth that he saw, it was the wide expanse of his own life since he first came to Abba Moussa that filled his vision. He offered up a prayer of praise unto the Heavenly Father for all of His care, then crossing himself, he jumped nimbly on Meshir's back and started off.

Meanwhile, Demiana saw a dream—was it a dream, or was she wide awake? She could not tell. All she knew was that she saw Guirguis riding Meshir towards the Mansion. So vivid was the scene before her eyes that she jumped out of bed, got dressed, and ran downstairs. As she reached the veranda, she stood stock still; sure enough, there was Guirguis on Meshir's back coming towards her. When he reached the steps, he jumped off his horse, leapt up to where she stood, and enfolded her in his arms. She put her hands around his face and passed them gently downwards, saying quietly, "Oh! It is you in flesh and blood indeed!"

"Of course it is I in flesh and blood. But how could you have been waiting for me when I sent no messenger ahead?"

She answered softly, "You sent no messenger... but who knows? Maybe it is Big Brother who did it. I saw you earlier this morning riding in the midst of the corn fields, and I rushed down to see—and there you were!" Resting her head on his breast, she sobbed quietly.

He waited for a few seconds, then putting his hand under her chin, he lifted her face up to him and said, "Now, is that how you greet me after such a long absence?"

She smiled, wiped her tears, then said as calmly as she could, "I am sobbing for joy! You see, this is the first time I've seen you since that fateful day. I heard of how they lashed you, and how courageous you were. I was filled with such conflicting emotions when I heard the story. Oh Guirguis, did they hurt you badly?" Her eyes filled with tears again.

He smiled and said, "They did their level best to hurt me, but I really can't describe to you the power that filled me. It flowed through my whole being, and I stood there almost enjoying myself. You were beside me, and so was Big Brother and Mariam. But that is a thing of the past, so let it go. Why dwell on it any longer?"

"I am glad it passed, and I promise not to mention it

again. I just couldn't help asking you about it now." She smiled radiantly and put her hands around his neck and said, "Welcome to Wissim, cousin Guirguis. Do come in." He walked with her into the sitting room, and they sat in a corner talking quietly until Abba Moussa appeared. As soon as they saw him, they came hastily towards him, greeting him and kissing his hand.

He looked at Guirguis for a while, then said, "Welcome my son. When did you come, and what brings you hither?" Guriguis told him everything, after which the holy man called for Pishoi and told him to have the guesthouse all ready, as they shall be having several visitors. Then turning to Guirguis, he said, "Every time I see you, you grow more in stature—and let me add, in wisdom and in grace too. Come, let us offer our prayer of thanksgiving , then you can have breakfast. Doubtless you are hungry."

"Famished, holy father."

All three of them went out and entered the church. When the prayers were ended, Abba Moussa told Demiana to take good care of Guirguis and to feed him generously while he went to see the needs of his people before the guests arrived.

***

The following morning, after singing the liturgy, a meeting was held in the church. Abba Moussa presided. All those who came discussed at length the different forms of persecutions which took place. Then some said that such a state of affairs could not last any longer, and that since neither diplomacy nor Christian tolerance bore any fruit, then war was the inevitable measure to be taken.

A hotheaded zealot stood up and said, "War! Let us declare war! In our present time, no person is immune, regardless of his rank or station. The holy Patriarch[54] is imprisoned three days because he cannot raise enough money to satisfy the greed of the ruler. Abba Moussa is mocked, and his gray beard is pulled by the rascal guards, though he is guest of the Wali. And that villain of a host keeps silent at their misdemeanor! The church dignitaries are scoffed at wherever they go, and the civilians are certainly more badly treated. Even Guirguis—who is supposed to be the favorite of the Wali—was scourged publicly. We cannot stand it any longer."

There were voices of assent. Abba Moussa listened in utter silence until all the voices were hushed, then he stood up saying, "My children, let it not be said of us that we waged war because we were not courageous enough to bear persecution. Our Blessed Savior could have called twelve legions of angels to kill those who dared lay hands on Him, but He refrained and suffered them to crucify Him, so that by His death He may give abundant life unto Man. He set for us an example, teaching us by deed and word what it means to live on earth as children of God. Then the disciples followed in His footsteps: 'They rejoiced that they were counted worthy to suffer shame for His Name.'[55] Are we not the descendants of those against whom emperor after emperor waged merciless persecutions? How did our fathers meet those persecutions? They neither fainted nor

---

54 Likely Pope Khail, the 46th Pope of Alexandria (see Appendix A).

55 Acts 5:41.

feared, and the only war they waged was their steadfast faith and joy at being tortured for our Lord's sake. Nay, St. Paul considered it a privilege, declaring that it is given to us so that we not only believe on Christ, but to also suffer with Him.[56] Therefore, I marvel at your behavior. Tell me Guirguis, when you were lashed, did it make you any less loved or respected amongst the men you lived with, even among those who are not of the faith?"

Here, Mena interrupted shouting, "Nay my holy father! Rather, it heightened his prestige, for they realized that he is even greater than they supposed him to be. None of you present here saw what happened."

Several voices exclaimed, "Tell us, tell us!"

Guirguis rose up smiling and said, "Brethren, I entreat you: keep to the main point and don't deviate into personal examples. For my part, I agree whole-heartedly with our most holy father that the experience did not hurt me in the least, and that because of it, I had the most comforting experience. This certainly would not have been my lot had I not been thus treated."

He sat and Abba Moussa resumed, "His beatitude the Patriarch felt very happy in prison. It gave him the chance to feel one with his people by experiencing the same tribulations. It was my privilege to share with him in his imprisonment—and what fruits of the Spirit it bore! I relate to you what I saw and experienced; I kept repeating to myself, who am I that I be counted worthy of being reviled for the Lord's name? Was not the Savior also mocked and scoffed at? If the Lord was thus treated, shall we not rejoice

---

56 Phil. 1:29

that we are counted worthy to receive the same treatment? Does not St. Paul make it plain in his epistles that is is a gift to suffer for Christ's sake? Therefore, consider my words and keep your eyes fixed upon Him who is the author and finisher of our faith. Strive to attain the measure of the stature of the fullness of Christ, who desires that we love our enemies and bless those that curse us." He went silent, looking into the face of each of those present by turn. Then blessing them with the sign of the cross, he sat down.

For a few minutes, everyone was silent. Then Youannis came forward, kissed the bishop's hand, turned around and said, "Holy fathers and brethren gathered here today, we took council to declare war, but perhaps it is wiser to consider the words of our father and try peaceful measures?"

A voice remonstrated, "Young man, do you not know that the only measures we have tried thus far were the measures of peace? And yet, they all failed."

"What about trying again?" interrupted Abba Moussa.

Again the remonstrator persisted, "Till when shall we try?"

Abba Moussa rejoined, "In His same manner: till seventy times seven."[57] Once more, silence ensued, and Youannis sat down.

Presently, the bishop of Thebes stood up. He was middle-aged, but so emaciated that he seemed old. A deep scar cut across his right cheek. He said, "You all know that I received this scar at the hands of soldiers, but since then, they have ceased to ill-treat me. Let us then ponder over the words of Abba Moussa. He is a man we all revere. We have

---

57 Matt. 18:22

seen how he has faced danger time and again, and we have swelled with pride when he stood undaunted in the defense of his children."

He sat down and a general discussion followed, but before any decision was taken, a messenger walked hastily in and delivered a letter to Abba Moussa, who gave it to Youannis to read. The letter was from the Caliph himself, ordering the taxes to be doubled and exacting a fine of twenty thousand gold dinars from the Patriarch. If these twenty thousand dinars were not paid within three days, the churches within the patriarchal see were to be ransacked.

As the reading ended, there was a tumult among those present, but Abba Moussa stood up and made the sign of the cross, at which complete silence was regained. The holy man said, "We will redouble our efforts—we will triple them if need be. We will strain them a hundredfold, but let it not be said of us that we betrayed our Savior and were unworthy children of the Blessed Martyrs. St. Paul said, 'Be angry and do not sin.'[58] It is quite natural for you to feel angry at these threats, but for the sake of our Savior, and the sublime line of blessed and saintly people who have lifted high the torch for us, let not your anger carry you to sin. Temper yourselves and remember that our Savior said, 'In your patience, possess ye your souls.'[59] Remember also, my children, that it is a great responsibility to be a Christian. It is the responsibility of being entrusted with the message of Christ and living up to it. How we fulfill this grand responsibility will allow the nations to see the Light of the Christ. Look out, then! Do not let the unbelievers blaspheme the blessed name of our

---

58 Eph. 4:26.

59 Luke 21:19.

Savior by our misdeeds instead of glorifying Him for our good works." Again, he blessed them and sat down.

Consequently, it was concluded that a few of them would be delegated to parley with the Wali, so that he would leave the churches in the event of not raising the demanded money. If the delegates failed, then war was to be declared. The leader unanimously chosen to be the head of the delegates was Abba Moussa, and if war was inevitable, then Youannis was to be the general. They shall all await his signal and follow his command.

After these conclusions, Abba Moussa once more stood up saying, "My children, I will gladly serve you, and I shall fervently pray that the New Man within you will have the upper hand, that you may joyfully accept the yoke of the Christ who said, 'In the world you shall have many tribulation, but be of good cheer; I have overcome the world.'"[60]

Then they all rose up and said the Lord's Prayer. After the benediction, they went out. The meeting had covered the space of two hours. It was almost twelve, but lunch was not to be served till one. Hence, they dispersed into groups; some ambling leisurely in the garden, some sipping the cool drinks offered to them as they sat on the verandah, others sat under the shade of the sycamore or by the brink of the river within the protection of the weeping willows.

Abba Moussa had detained Guirguis and Youannis, so Demiana took Mena separately into a corner of the spacious living room and asked him to relate to her what happened on the memorable day of the lashing. Mena was

---

60 John 16:33.

only too delighted to describe it to her, to the minutest detail, the event with great enthusiasm. She listened to him quite entranced. He had barely finished his recital—and Demiana's cheeks were still wet with tears—when the holy man appeared with both Youannis and Guirguis on either side of him. Demiana did not try to hide her tears, and Mena's face was flushed as the three men approached.

Guirguis turned to Youannis and said, "By the blessed Mother of God, Mena was relating to Demiana..."

He stopped short, for Demiana came forward to him, her tears flowing again, and said, "Yes, he did tell me all about it. But it was at my request that he did it. You made me promise not to mention it to you, but you did not forbid me to ask Mena, did you? After all, I have a right to know, don't I, holy father?"

"Of course you do." The old man patted her affectionately on the shoulder.

She wiped her tears and smiled quite happily saying, "Now I am content, and I give thanks unto my God and unto the Blessed Mother that you have behaved in such a worthy manner, my Guirguis."

***

A number of those who came to Wissim left soon after lunch. The few who stayed left early the next day. The only ones who remained behind were Youannis, Mena, and Guirguis. Together, with Demiana, they sat at the feet of Abba Moussa, discussing the current situation from every possible angle. The holy father was unwavering in his plea for peace and his condemnation of war; in his sight, war was a blasphemy against the God of Love. Demiana and Guirguis gave him their wholehearted support, but the two brothers were not quite convinced; they both thought that war might be a good remedy when other means failed.

The old man, in his almost limitless patience, asked, "And what happens if we are defeated?"

Youannis gave a swift reply: "We shall not be defeated. There is so much righteous indignation among us, and such a readiness to sacrifice, that we will surely be made victors."

"If such qualities were consecrated for peace, then we would be more than victors."

This private meeting lasted until dinner. During the meal, the holy man directed the conversation towards personal matters, asking about the different members of the family, and especially about the two sons of Youannis. When dinner was ended, they all decided that they were to give themselves to the pleasant task of reliving their earlier days; they had but a few short hours before they were to leave in the early morning. Guirguis and Demiana went out and sat on the soft earth under the sycamore tree just as they were wont to do, and thus they refreshed their memories and renewed their spirits. They sat together, oblivious of time, until Mena came and apologetically reminded Guirguis that it was almost dawn, and that they were preparing to leave.

The couple had a hearty laugh at his awkward manner, and Guirguis said, "Right you are. Kindly fetch Meshir for me." When Mena went to do his bidding, Demiana and Guirguis stood up. For a few short seconds, they stood silent, watching the Nile serenely flowing by, then they looked into each other's eyes. Everything around about them was suggestive of serenity: the Nile, the ripe rich corn stalks swaying ever so gently under the light breeze, the clear azure above with the sun already shooting its rays across the sky. Peace filled the whole scene and invaded their hearts.

Demiana said, "It is all so serene and beautiful. I am thankfully happy for these few hours. I do not know when we shall meet again, but I know that greater trials await us all, and especially you, because of your situation. Yet I am confident that 'He who has begun a good work in you will perform it.'[61] I shall always pray for you. If ever my human frailty gets the better of me, I will remind myself of all the hours of strength and invisible support accorded to us by the Father, as well as by the strong power of our love."

"Excellent, my dearest one." He enfolded her within his arms and kissed her just as Mena came within view.

Then, as he was about to mount, she put her arm around Meshir's neck, patted him softly and said, "O Meshir, you have been an ever-faithful friend. Bear Guirguis well, and may you be swiftest at the hour of need." Guirguis again kissed her and jumped on Meshir, who started off instantly. She stood and watched Guirguis and her two brothers as they galloped off, then slipped into the church for a short while.

***

Guirguis and his two cousins hardly spoke a word on their journey, as each was so wrapped up in his own thoughts.

---

61 Phil. 1:6.

On their arrival, they found Shenouti pacing up and down by the gate of the Coptic quarter; no sooner had he espied them than he ran towards Guirguis exclaiming, "Thank God you have come! The Wali has returned about an hour ago and has sent for you."

"Very good," answered Guirguis, "I shall go to him straightaway." Then turning to his cousins, he said, "It may be wiser that you go home now, while I see what the reason is for this quick behest." They agreed, and Guirguis gave his order to Meshir to run swiftly, so that within a few minutes, Guirguis was walking into the private living room of the Wali. He laughed quite joyfully, and greeted him saying, "Welcome home, my lord."

The Wali answered, "I see that you have played truant and ran off from Al-Fustat, for I sent for you as soon as I arrived, and you kept me waiting for a whole hour before making and appearance. What sort of punishment do you deserve now?"

Guirguis laughed and said, "In truth, my lord, I did leave the city. But here I come and you can deal with me as you like—only don't be too hard a school-master."

"Well come, then, take your seat, and tell me a few short tales."

Guirguis made swift reply, 'No, you must tell me all about your journey," and thus sat down.

The Wali said, "Is that the punishment you deserve for being late?"

Guirguis laughed quite naturally again, answering, "Nay, not so, my lord. I just want to know how you fared on your journey, that I may better choose my tales."

The Wali then told him that it was quite a pleasant journey, and that they were all the guests of the Abbot of the monastery at Al-Quosier, who entertained them quite regally.

Guirguis interposed, "And is it because of that that you are asking for twenty thousand dinars?"

"We have to stop the mouths of the hungry wolves at our doors."

"What! By turning wolves on us?"

"There is no alternative for us."

"You can ask for the money graciously, without threatening."

An hour later, Guirguis rode out of the palace. He had come to terms with the Wali and was feeling quite elated in anticipation of the results of the meeting which he had arranged between Abba Moussa and the Wali. He rode home with a smile on his lips and dreamy eyes. Maybe, after all, he and Demiana could get married sooner than they thought.

Arriving home, he ran in to give the pleasant news, and they were all very delighted.

Early the next day, Youannis went to the Patriarch and gave him a detailed account of what had taken place. The Successor of Saint Mark[62] was rather upset to find Youannis among the supporters of war, reproved him, and reminded him that it is incompatible with Christ's teaching. While he was thus talking, Abba Moussa himself walked in. He

---

62 St. Mark the Evangelist is the founder of Christianity in Egypt, and he is the Coptic Church's first pope. As such, every Coptic Pope thereafter is his successor.

had come to meet the Wali, as it had been decided. The two fathers of the church had a short talk; they both held firm to the principle of God's Fatherhood and man's brotherhood, and accordingly denounced war most emphatically. While they were talking quietly, a messenger had been sent from the Wali asking for an audience, and he came in to tell Abba Moussa that he could go immediately. So the bishop left, asking the patriarch to pray for him.

The Wali greeted the bishop with great deference and related to him at length all that had happened at Al-Quosier. He added that for his part, he was ready to make things easier, but the Caliph was in need of money to pay off the rising upstarts. For the sake of the Abbot of el-Quoseir, he was not going to insist on the money being brought within three days, nor was he going to touch any church. He only asked Abba Moussa to use his influence with his people and make them pay the necessary money in as short a time as possible.

Guirguis was of course present during all this talk, and he did not fail to put in a little spice. The old bishop promised to give the money to the Wali, and both men took leave of each other in the friendliest of terms.

The same afternoon, the Wali, to prove his new good will, went and paid a visit to the Patriarch with a number of his courtiers, and he paid him homage before them all. This visit inaugurated a period of friendly relations, during which no insult or persecution to the Copts went unpunished. They, in their turn, paid the necessary money in a week's time and gave the new tax quite willingly.

But alas, this period of peace and good will lasted but for the space of three short months. It was a Friday afternoon, and one of the hottest days of June—so much so, that it brought back to the memory of Guirguis in a fantastic fashion that afternoon on which Big Brother came home wounded to death. The memory roused strange forebodings within his breast, which he vainly tried to dispel. He endeavored to belie his inward restlessness by an extra outward joviality, but in spite of his endeavors, his attempts at joviality were interrupted with lapses of ominous silence. During one of these lapses, the Wali felt so alarmed that he asked Guirguis if he was unwell. The question brought Guirguis to a fuller realization of his inward state in sharp contrast with his outward show. For the space of a few seconds, he forgot those around, and had his faraway look in his eyes. He saw, once more, Big Brother entrusting him with the task of bearing the torch. All those around him suddenly became very silent, eyeing him somewhat fearfully. The complete silence which reigned for a few seconds brought him to himself, and he gave answer to the Wali. Yet his answer was somewhat vague. The Wali looked alarmed. After a few more minutes of silence, Guirguis realized that once more, he must summon all his powers, not only to overcome his own inward disquiet, but also to dispel the gloom that seemed to invade all those around him. He invoked the help of the Blessed Virgin and all the saints, and summoned to his memory the picture of Demiana as she bade him godspeed at Wissim, recalling her words, "If ever my human frailty get the better of me, I shall remind myself of all the strength and the invisible support accorded to us by the Fathers, as well as by the strong power of our love." With these thoughts and memories, he fortified himself. Presently, he was talking and laughing in his most charming matter. In a short while, the Wali and his courtiers were also laughing and talking as hilariously as ever.

Suddenly, like a bolt out of the blue, a messenger ran into their midst, chilling them and dispelling their merriment. The messenger went straight to the Wali, made obeisance, then handed him a letter. The Wali, in turn, gave it to Guirguis to read. It was from the Caliph, and it described how the new faction was gaining ground each day and becoming a real menace. Therefore, more money was needed, and a general mobilization was to be declared in case war became a necessity. Above all, money had to be raised at whatever cost.

Guirguis read the letter in slow clear measures. As he read it, the restlessness within him became explainable. When he ended his reading, he gave the letter to the Wali, who folded it and opened it again and again, feeling at a loss. Guirguis regained his self-mastery before anyone else and said, "Well, my lord, we are not going to fold our arms and sit back while the enemy is gaining ground. We must be up and doing. We have brain and brawn, so why worry or hesitate? The letter is clear; money is needed as well as men, and you can master both."

His words were uttered with great calm and confidence, thus infusing the Wali with new strength. He said, "By Allah, you are worth your weight in gold, Guirguis."

Guirguis laughingly retorted, "That is a goodly sum," and his laughter was contagious. A little later, the Wali took Guirguis aside and reviewed with him all the possibilities for meeting the demands of the Caliph. Guirguis gave his word of honor that he will ask his people to pay as much as they could. The Wali was relieved at this assurance and in turn, promised that he will not permit any insult to the

Copts to pass unpunished. Thus the commotion roused by the Caliph's messenger was not felt outside the narrow circle of the Wali and his courtiers. And apart from the money that had to be paid, the Copts still enjoyed greater freedom and continued friendliness. Yet, there was a growing feeling of tension, for almost every day, fresh alarming news of the rising faction reached them.

Another month passed, during which the Copts, though enjoying freedom and amicability, were strained to their utmost financially. Then another messenger arrived, and his message spelled pessimism and war. There was no other alternative now, for the new faction was already marching towards Damascus and the Caliph had to leave the city, so money had to be sent in all haste.

It so happened that when this second messenger came, Guirguis was absent. The Wali, to prove his good will, gave him a three days' leave, which he didn't hesitate to spend at Wissim.

The jealous courtiers seized their chance; the first one said, "Surely, those accursed infidels can afford more money than they pay."

A second added, "It is only your indulgence that encourages them."

A third continued, "Don't you know yet that they are wily? Test them. Throw their Patriarch in prison, together with that man called Abba Moussa, and see how quickly they will open their coffers and pay you in an instant." With these and other remarks, they prevailed in pressuring the Wali to follow the course of tyranny. Fearing lest he waiver at sight of Guirguis, they convinced him to take active measures immediately. So a messenger was hastily sent to summon the Patriarch to their presence. When he came, he was told amid jeers and jibes that he either paid a hundred thousand dinars immediately, or be thrown into prison. Abba Moussa was on tour in his see, so he was away from Wissim.

When Shenouti ran to give Guirguis the news of the imprisonment, Guirguis was confounded. "God in heaven! I have never had so much as an hour's respite, and when I do get a holiday, such a dreadful event takes place! Oh the unguarded moments! The need for continuous vigil! Mother of God, come to our rescue!" Thus he raved as one in a delirium.

Demiana gently put her hand on his arm and said, "You are still the favorite of the Wali. I am sure that when you go and speak to him, he will release our venerable Father."

"Demiana my love, sometimes I feel the burden is getting a little too heavy for me to bear."

She smiled and said, "But you have such big square shoulders, you ought to thank our Heavenly Father for them. Yet don't think that you bear the burden alone; less square shoulders help you along in your struggle."

He looked into her smiling face and radiant eyes, then tenderly passed his hand over her hair and said, "A worthy daughter of your forebears indeed. Yet, who would say that such words of strength could be uttered by such a fragile mouth! But then, you have always been a source of strength to me since we were children, since the day I told you about Big Brother." He kissed her, then said, "And now, I must rush back to the lion's den. I won't be able to bid Abba Moussa goodbye, so please kiss his hand for me and ask him to pray for us, one and all."

She said, "Just wait a minute till I run and fetch you something to eat on the way. It is noon, and you ate nothing since breakfast."

"No, no, it is no time to eat now. I can refresh myself when I have fulfilled my sacred errand." Rushing downstairs, he hastened to the stable, jumped on Meshir's back, and galloped at top speed. This time, he made the entire journey on horseback, for the boat was too slow a conveyance at the moment. As he sped along, a voice persistently iterated within him, "Greater tribulations are in store, gather therefore all your forces to stand the test bravely to the end." The galloping of the horse seemed to keep rhythm with these words as he hastened on.

In less than an hour, he crossed the gate of the Wali's palace, and within a few minutes, he walked into the dining room as the Wali and his courtiers were having a late lunch. No sooner did he appear than silence reigned, and as he came forward to salute the Wali, the latter said immediately, and somewhat coldly, "You still have another day's holiday. I thought you were away from Al-Fustat, so why this unpleasant surprise?"

Guirguis looked him squarely, then looked at each of the courtiers by turn and said in very measured accents, "The unpleasant surprise came from you, I assure you, for it never occurred to me that you could so easily forget your promises and your friendship and listen to the counsel of small men." His right hand held firmly to the cross on his breast, while his eyes searched his hearers very intently.

They colored at the intensity of his gaze, and only the Wali answered, "Listen, war is not a game. The caliph is already engaged in a struggle that may cost him his throne.

We, as loyal subjects, must pay him the necessary money immediately, for we cannot afford to lose time."

"But you always got the money you wanted. You can imprison me as you once did, but I see no reason why you should imprison the foremost among us, one who is venerated even by you for his wisdom."

"Listen Guirguis, 'all is fair in love and war,' and since we are at war, the surest way of obtaining the money is to imprison the highest man among the Copts, because both your veneration and your love for him will surely make you hasten to pay what is demanded of you."

"And if we refuse to pay the money before you release our Pope?"

"Are you threatening?"

"I have threatened but once, when you ordered my beating. Do you remember? And my warning came true. Now I threaten again, because I know my people. After all, human patience has a limit, so be careful and do not strain this limit."

Here, some courtiers seemed to have overcome the fears roused in them at sight of Guirguis, and several voices clamored, "He dares to fling such words at you and you don't punish him."

"Imprison him!"

"Confiscate his land!"

"Banish him to some desert island!"

The Wali suddenly got infuriated "Silence, all of you! Am I not the master here? Do I have to take orders from you? You all know full well that Guirguis is my friend, and he is the only one who can ever cheer me up and make me forget the worries of the state. Isn't it enough that I accepted your counsel to imprison the venerable father?" With these words, silence fell on all of them.

Guirguis took a step towards the Wali, then said, "Now that's a true friend. Come now and hear some of the tales I have collected for you."

"Come sit by my side and recount them to me."

"I will, but before I start, graciously order the release of the venerable father."

The Wali was silent, while angry mutterings sounded from the courtiers, at which the Wali raised his head and answered, "I cannot release him. I have sworn by the Caliph's head that he will remain in prison till the money I asked for is paid."

Guirguis again looked at the Wali and his courtiers with intensity, then he looked away from them. For a few minutes, he seemed remote from them just as he would do from time to time, and fear gripped the hearts of the onlookers whenever he was in such a state. Meanwhile, in his mind's eye, different images succeeded one after the other. He could very easily refuse to sit by the Wali as his favorite courtier and abandon the task of acting as bulwark to his people, but this thought brought in its wake the picture of the miseries that will ensue by the triumph of those very courtiers sitting before him, plotting his own downfall and the slavery of his people. Then the strong persistent call of love and devotion rang in his ears: the last plea of Big Brother, the gentle but enthusing influence of Abba Moussa, the love of Demiana—all these infused him with new strength.

He brought himself back to the presence of the Wali and his courtiers. He laughed and took his seat beside the Wali, which was always left vacant in his absence, then said, "Here I come to you famished, and you sit back and stare at me without asking me to eat. Now is that fair, my lord?"

The Wali heaved a sigh of relief, while his courtiers muttered again unintelligibly. The former said, "By Allah, you puzzle me, man. I don't know with whom you commune! I confess that I feel frightened when I behold you preferring the company of the unseen to that of the seen. But by Allah, I like you and feel your absence very heavily. Come, wile away my worries by some of your charming conversations."

Guirguis ate his usual frugal fare, talking about various subjects except the one nearest to his heart. He had to stay at court far into the night, refusing to cede his ground. When finally the Wali retired and each of the courtiers went his way, he left on Meshir's back. Standing by the gate, and lifting up his eyes to the clear sky—so beautiful with its myriad of stars—his heart rose up in an earnest plea coupled with a song of adoration. He recalled Demiana's words reminding him of his broad shoulders and the invisible help accorded to him. Then talking to Meshir he said, "We must make a different pilgrimage tonight, my trusty friend, before going home." Setting his face towards the prison, he rode off in haste in spite of the late hour.

The Patriarch was still awake and received him with open arms. Guirguis, throwing off all guise, kissed the old man's hand again and again, while his tears flowed down his cheeks like a little child. Then mastering himself, he said, "Forgive me, holy father, for it seems to me that had I been present when the messengers of evil arrived, I could have spared you this imprisonment."

The venerable Father smiled in his kindly manner and said, "Do you remember, my son, what our Blessed Savior said to his disciples when they asked Him why the man was born blind? 'Neither hath this man sinned nor his parents, but that the works of God should be made manifest in him.'[63] Therefore, you are not to blame, for you certainly could not have foreseen such a thing. Besides, we are God's ambassadors in chains, as St. Paul declared."[64] Guirguis proceeded to tell the Patriarch what happened to him when he met the Wali, then the venerable Father placed his hand on his head to bless, absolve, and send him away in peace.

Henceforth, Guirguis would go daily to the dark hole in which the Patriarch was imprisoned the first thing in the morning and the last thing at night. He would see to his needs and the needs of those imprisoned with him, bearing with him the prayers of the people and carrying back the papal message of hope and courage to the believers.

Twelve days later, Abba Moussa returned to Wissim. It was after sunset, so Demiana gave strict injunctions to all those living about the Mansion to keep silent concerning the Patriarch until the morning. Early the next day, she went down to wait on the old man herself. When he asked her why she came down so early, she replied, "Well, I have news to tell you—not exactly pleasant news."

He smiled and patted her on the shoulder, saying, "My daughter, don't worry. You want to tell me that our beloved Patriarch is in prison." Seeing her surprise, he continued, "I

---

63 John 9:3.

64 Eph. 6:20.

PE KHAIL
TH POPE
OF
EXANDRIA

saw it in a dream last night," then added, "I am forewarned by the Spirit that bonds and afflictions will abide in me. So during my absence, you must look after everybody here and consider yourself the guide to those around you." She opened her lips to say something, but he put his hand on her shoulder, smiled into her eyes, and said, "We must all be ready at anytime for whatever is laid upon us. Think of the heavy yoke put on the shoulders of Guirguis, and think of how valiantly he is carrying it. You must be the valiant partner to so valiant a man."

She kissed his hands, then said in a voice that was barely above a whisper, "I shall do my best to be worthy of your confidence and his valor."

With these words, Abba Moussa gave her his blessings and departed.

That very afternoon, he appeared at the court of the Wali. The latter got up to meet him and welcomed him with reverence. The old bishop accepted his welcome quite graciously, but no sooner was he seated than he immediately reproached the Wali for imprisoning the Patriarch. The Wali was adamant on this subject, and once more repeated to the bishop what he said before to Guirguis, adding, "It would be easier for me to imprison you than release him."

At these words, Guirguis started as one stung, but Abba Moussa nodded to him smilingly, thus silencing him. Then he said quietly, but firmly, "Most welcome to me is such an imprisonment. I pray you order your soldiers to accompany me there, lest the people seeing me going alone will block my way—not only my people, but yours as well."

The Wali was taken aback; he did not expect this answer, though he had more than once seen the bishop's frank courage and inflexibility. He stood up and raised his hand in remonstration.

The bishop smiled indulgently. Keeping an eye on Guirguis all along, he said, "Come, be a man of action. You seem to be frightened at the import of your own words, but the cup must overflow."

The Wali answered, "I cannot understand what you say."

"But surely you understand that you threatened to imprison me, and that I willingly accepted to go to prison. Isn't that enough for you?" The eyes of Guirguis implored his beloved bishop, who continued to smile to him, thus soothing him in silence. Meanwhile, the Wali sat down, clapped his hands for his bodyguard, then ordered him to have a group of soldiers ready to accompany Abba Moussa to prison. The guard bowed and disappeared.

When Abba Moussa had come in, he originally took his seat beside the Wali on the other side of Guirguis. Now Guirguis could not contain himself any longer; he pulled a low circular leather cushion and sat at the feet of his beloved spiritual father. He took his old wrinkled hand in both of his and said in a low voice, "Holy father, have pity on me! I cannot see you in this black hole, I shall be in agony..."

The old man put his free hand on the young man's head and said very tenderly, "Guirguis, my son, do you remember how St. Anthony, living in the vastness of the desert and enjoying the ecstasy of God's presence, left his solitude and went to Alexandria when he heard of the persecutions waged by Maximianus? Why did he plunge into the melee? To share with his children their sorrows and their tribulations. Would you have me prefer to go free when others are being sorely tried?"

ⲡⲓⲛⲓϣϯ
ⲁⲃⲃⲁ ⲁⲛⲧⲱⲛⲓ

ST. ANTHONY
THE GREAT

Guirguis only kissed the hand of Abba Moussa in answer, and still held it between his two. Presently, the bodyguard entered to say that the soldiers were at the door. Abba Moussa got up, and so did Guirguis, who said, "Allow me to accompany you, father."

The bishop put his hand on the shoulder of Guirguis and said, "No my son, not now." His eyes spoke volumes to the eyes of Guirguis in just the space of a few short seconds.

Guirguis again kissed the hand he held, then bowed his head saying, "Bless me, my father."

The old man put his hand on the young man's head and gave his blessing in silence. Then turning to the bodyguard, he said, "Lead on." Guirguis followed him with his eyes until he disappeared, then went to the window and looked on until the escort and the escorted went out of sight. After that, he turned around and came back quietly and slowly to his seat beside the Wali. For a few minutes silence reigned, then Guirguis brought himself back to his talk with a superman effort. In a short while, the Wali and his courtiers were enlivened by his conversation as though nothing had happened, so much so that some of them whispered among themselves, "What man is this! And what powers does he possess to be able to master himself so rapidly? For surely his heart is bleeding, yet who can detect the wound when he sees him now?" And they felt more jealous and more awed.

***

Guirguis was indeed sorely wounded, but he valiantly conversed and laughed. To spite him, the courtiers joined the Wali in asking for more anecdotes and more jokes until well after midnight. When the Wali finally did retire and release him, Guirguis went out, whistled to Meshir and mounted him. Then patting his horse, he said, "Well Meshir, we go to fulfill a doubly sacred task. We have the pleasure of Abba Moussa's nearness, but God above, we surely did not want him to be in such a hole."

Meshir started off at a gallop, feeling his master's zeal to be there rapidly. Arriving at the dark hole in which the two most outstanding Prelates of the church were confined, he got off and ran unto them, kissing their hands by turn.

Before saying a word, the Patriarch said, "Guirguis my son, truly yours is the heavier burden."

"Oh holy father, it is indeed an agony for me to see you in this terrible place—so dark, so narrow, and so suffocating. I would rather have been scourged time and agin than see you in so filthy a hole."

Abba Moussa put out his hand to feel for Guirguis, placed it on his shoulder, and said in a voice that filled Guirguis with unutterable peace, "My son, you are being scourged daily for our sake, and for the sake of your people, though no lash falls on your broad shoulders. The Loving Father in heaven fill you with His strength by the prayers of our Blessed Lady and all the saints."

**

The following night, when Guirguis had fulfilled his usual pilgrimage to the imprisoned and went home, he found a messenger from Youannis who told him that they have decided to declare war. Those who had confided in the leadership of Youannis were just awaiting his signal to move, and he came to the conclusion that war was the only way of meeting the present situation. The password he chose was "Abba Moussa," at which Guirguis laughed outright saying, "The irony of it! Using the name of our beloved bishop as a sign of war when he is absolutely against it, as you all know. 'Meshir' would certainly be more to the point. Yet, one more plea I will send to you, my dear cousin." He sat down in spite of the late hour and penned a message in which he pleaded the cause of peace, reminding Youannis of the fact that the two venerable Fathers in prison were whole-heartedly for peace and considered war as a blasphemy against God's holy will. When the message was ended, the messenger took it and returned immediately to Samanoud.

It was dawn by the time he arrived there, but already several leaders were gathered; they were all moved by the same events, though none had any contact with the other! The messenger delivered the message of Guirguis to Youannis, who read it aloud. When he finished reading, they all protested and unanimously upheld Youannis in his stand for war. So they decided that, in spite of the plea of Guirguis, and as much as they would have liked to obey the wishes of the Patriarch and Abba Moussa, yet in face of all the events, they will declare war. The march was to start simultaneously from different directions. It was the 25th of Thoth. Each of those present was to rush back to his province, because on the 30th of Thoth, Youannis was to march in force in Al-Fustat, and they were all to do the same simultaneously. The password would still be 'Abba Moussa.' Wissa, the trusted attendant of Youannis, was sent to carry his message to all the provinces, so that whoever preferred to join may do so.

Having thus come to a decision, each departed at a different hour, so as not to route suspicion.

Wissa first went to Guirguis and passed on to him the message, then continued his journey. Guirguis took all the necessary measures; no woman, child, or old person was to go out beyond the gates of the Coptic quarter, while all the men were to be alert and on guard. Inside their own town, they were not to start any broil, but be only on the defensive. Those who wanted to take part in the war must go and join forces with Youannis. Having taken all the necessary precautions for the safety of those within his domain, he sent Shenouti in haste to Wissim with a message to Demiana reminding her of her own words, that at the hour of our greatest need, God's grace abounds, for "man's extremity is God's opportunity." Commending her to the protection of the blessed Virgin and all the saints, he added, "We shall all be praying for each other."

That night, when he went to visit the illustrious prisoners, he sat at their feet in silence for a good long while. Abba Moussa, who had loved Guirguis at first sight and whose love for him grew with the years, sensed the unuttered agony within his soul. He lay his hand on the head of Guirguis, and for sometime, prayed in silence. Then he said, "My son, within three weeks' time, a new dawn shall break. My greatest sympathy is with you in particular, for yours is the hardest task. But remember that the more privileged you are, the more is demanded of you. Our Heavenly Father has blessed you with many talents, and by His Grace, you are trading valiantly with them. Meanwhile, you must remember that for the time being, you are the Wali's favorite. Keep up my son, however difficult; the prayers of the saints and His beloved sustain you unto the end."

Guirguis could only kiss the hands of the venerable father in silence; the tumult within his heart was too strong for words.

***

On the last day of the month of Thoth, as the first rays of the sun shot across the eastern sky, Youannis started his offensive as the head of his men. His wife had also pleaded with him to obey the fathers, expressing the strange forebodings which filled her soul with fears. Yet, he waived away her fears with the same cocksureness with which he spoke to Abba Moussa.

As soon as he started his move toward Al-Fustat, his courier was sent to the Wali with the declaration of war. When the Wali received it, he colored, then turned pale, saying "By Allah, this is the most unexpected. Who would have thought that the accursed infidels would take such action?"

His courtiers clamored for the head of Guirguis, while he sat with his imperturbable smile. Though the Wali was infuriated by the Copts, he was still fond of Guirguis. The clamor of his courtiers infuriated him all the more. "Get out of my sight, all of you!" he stormed, "I have told you more than once that my best friend is Guirguis. See what your counsel has brought!" Thus they were silenced. Calling for his bodyguard, he ordered him to carry the declaration of war to the general of the troops. When the bodyguard disappeared, he turned once more on his courtiers and said,

"Either you keep your mouths shut or you go away. I will tolerate no man today."

One faint voice murmured, "Except for Guirguis."

The Wali said with violence, "Hold your tongue, you fainthearted coward! Had you been a man, you would have stood up and openly said your words instead of wily murmuring it. And you're right; with the exception of Guirguis who towers over you all, leave." Complete silence ensued.

This commotion gave Guirguis enough time to quiet the tumult within his heart, and having complete control over himself, he said most suavely, "Now, may I complete the story I began, my lord?"

"Yes, by all means do." When Guirguis terminated his tale, the Wali said, "By Allah, I like you more than ever, yet I don't know why! Sometimes I feel as though I ought to kill you and finish with you! Then, I suddenly remember all that has passed between us, and how you are still the only man who can soothe away my heartaches. Surely, you must have had a magician for a teacher."

Guirguis laughed quietly. He sat quite erect and looked with confident triumph around him, then he lay back and said weightily, "Maybe I did have a magician for a teacher after all."

***

For five days the battle raged, and every day the Coptic army steadily advanced. The courtiers kept silent, not daring even to glance at Guirguis, who seemed to gain more and more power over the Wali in spite of all odds.

On the morning of the sixth day, as Guirguis was walking out of prison after his morning mission to go to the Wali, he espied Zoheir amidst the crowds on the streets and noticed that the latter tried to evade him, for he slunk away, and in no time disappeared. At this slimy action, the heart of Guirguis suddenly leapt within his breast with frightful forebodings. Why should this man—this cousin of his—reappear at Al-Fustat just now? He urged Meshir onward.

When he reached the gate of the palace, Shenouti was waiting for him as usual. He said to him, "Shenouti, Zoheir is in our town this morning. My heart tells me he is up to some evil. Your job is to find out where he is and to keep track of him. But he is very cautious."

That very evening, Shenouti came in a little after sunset. His face spoke plainly to Guirguis, who seized the first chance and went out for a few minutes to see him.

No sooner were the two men alone than Shenouti said, "Your heart was right. Zoheir has come here to betray us. He learned the password, and with it, has mingled with our men. I heard him talking with one of the courtiers, and gathered that he told him who the leader is and where his exact position lies."

Guirguis clutched at the cross on his breast exclaiming, "Holy Mother of God! Shenouti, my trusty friend, jump on Meshir's back and rush immediately to Youannis to warn him. Hurry, we cannot afford to wait." The two men embraced each other, each commending the other to God's protection, and parted.

Guirguis stood alone under the open sky breathing a

prayer, then said aloud, "Courage, dear heart. The new day is not far off." Then he walked with measured steps to his place beside the Wali once more.

As for Shenouti, he galloped off as fast as Meshir could run; never had Meshir been so nimble as on that memorable evening. Yet, more than once, Shenouti had to slacken his pace and proceed warily, as he sensed Meshir's mane bristling. All through the night he rode.

Then, just as the stars were paling and the first heralds of dawn were about to proclaim the new day, three riders barred Shenouti's way and challenged him. Shenouti had no choice in the matter, so he fought with all the zeal of his heart. Two of his opponents fell. Then Meshir gave way, but still, Shenouti fought on. Finally, he succeeded in dealing a deadly blow to his last opponent, who fell down. He, himself, was bleeding from several wounds dealt to him. Nonetheless, when he saw that his foes had all fallen, he seemed unaware of his own state. The one obsessing thought which mastered him was to deliver the message, for he was very near to the camp of Youannis.

He ran on, until he was within hearing of the general. Feeling too weak to take another step, he mustered all of his remaining strength and shouted, "We are betrayed, General Youannis! Beware!"

Then he fell down dead.

Chapter Four

The Unconquerable Buoyancy of the Human Soul

Youannis had awakened just a few minutes before Shenouti's warning. He always woke up at dawn, but now as he sat in his tent, he could not yet realize the significance of what had happened. He got up and went to where Shenouti lay, bent over him, and felt him just to convince himself that it was not mere hallucinations. Then the words of the dead man echoed and reechoed in his head.

For a few minutes he seemed transfixed, after which his well-trained ear detected the sound of horses' hoofs coming from a distance. Immediately, he stood up, lifted up a curtain, and took up his trumpet, which he blew in full blast. No sooner had he blown it than he snatched his shield and his sword and rushed out. Some of his men hastened to his side, but before they had fully assembled, the foes were upon them and engaged them in a fierce battle.

From dawn till dusk, the battle raged. The enemy forces poured in endless numbers; the few who were with Youannis were completely surrounded. It was a desperate battle, but neither Youannis nor his men gave way; they fought with great might. As the sun was setting, Youannis himself fell. Those who still had the strength to fight continued on. By sunset, not a single man of them was alive, for even the wounded were finished off.

***

When Guirguis went on his nightly visit to the venerable fathers, he found that some ruffians had stormed the dark hole and were beating and reviling them. They gave Abba Moussa double share of the abuse, for it was his name that was taken as password. Immediately, he returned to the Wali, despite the late hour. Of course, the sentinels let him pass without any question. He ran upstairs, straight to the private quarters, and knocked.

When the Wali heard his voice, he hastily asked, "What ails you, Guirguis? Come in."

"Much," answered Guirguis, pushing the door and walking in. He described to the Wali what he saw by the torchlight, adding, "And all this for no reason except that it was rumored that 'Abba Moussa' was the password." The voice of Guirguis vibrated with his emotions which he vainly endeavored to master; it found an echo in the heart of his hearer, to the extent that he ordered his own guards to rush to the prison, arrest the malefactors, and thrash them in the morning in the public square.

The following day, it was proclaimed all over the land that General Youannis was slain with all his chosen men. At this proclamation, a reign of terror started—men, women, and children were massacred on the streets; houses and fields were set on fire; looting, pillaging, and rioting became the rule of the day; guerrilla fights took place in every province. Only two spots were still respected amidst all this woe and strife: the Mansion at Wissim and the Coptic quarter at Al-Fustat. For in spite of all the hatred and malice poured on the Copts all over the land, and in spite of the continued imprisonment of the Patriarch and Abba Moussa, the Wali still loved Guirguis and still favored him, kept him at his side, and for his sake, he gave strict orders concerning these two spots. Guirguis kept firm his ground at a mighty cost, and succeeded in showing a calm and unruffled front. To all onlookers, and especially to the courtiers, he seemed untouched or even unaware that his cousin was slain and his kinsmen were defeated. Meanwhile, he succeeded in convincing the Wali to send provisions to the imprisoned and to gradually stop his men from killing and looting.

Ten days later, an earthquake shook the whole land, from the shores of the Mediterranean to the borders of Aswan. Guirguis found it propitious to tell the Wali that Allah was angry at his behavior. The latter was so convinced of this that he ordered the release of the Patriarch, Abba Moussa and all others with them. He also sent his messenger all over the land giving strict orders that anyone caught molesting a Copt shall be duly punished.

While Guirguis thus strove, Mena could not even venture outside his room. The blow of Youannis's death dazed him. In vain did Mariam try to soothe him by word and example; she did her utmost. Consequently, she decided to shield away Guirguis from his cousin's despairing attitude. That was not so difficult, for Guirguis went down early and came back late.

As soon as she heard that the venerable prelates were released, she sent them a message describing Mena's inconsolability and despair. Thereupon, Pishoi was sent to summon Mena to Abba Moussa, who was residing with his Patriarch at *Al-Muallakah* Church. Naturally, Mena hastened to obey. The serenity that flooded the two men of God gradually pervaded Mena's soul. Without words, he found himself slowly regaining his equilibrium and his faith.

The amnesty declared came a little too late. For two days, a courtier arrived early morning bearing the disconcerting news that the rising faction reached Palestine and was continuing its march towards Syria. The Caliph Marwan was retreating in all haste, leaving Damascus for Al-Fustat in the hope that he will find succor in Egypt. At these news, consternation seized all those present. The Wali turned questioning eyes to Guirguis. Guirguis returned his gaze, and his eyes at that moment betrayed all the anguish of his heart, then he looked away from him and into the distance. Silence fell, and the same sense of awe filled the courtiers.

Then Guirguis spoke in low measured tones that none but the Wali could hear, saying, "Our beloved country is sorely wounded. Some of her best men have fallen these last days. Had Youannis been spared, he would have come to the rescue. But.." He paused, then looked at the courtiers who were all sitting in gloomy silence. He got up from his seat and walked around, gazing into the faces of those who had advised the imprisonment of the Patriarch, and who later found an alley in the traitor Zoheir. His eyes were like live coals as he fixed them on each by turn. They quaked before his gaze.

His hand firmly gripped the cross on his breast. Then he stood in their midst, and again he spoke, this time his voice shook the hall, "Little did you gauge the result of your evil counsel. You were blind to everything save the one aim of humiliating me and my people and turning the heart of the Wali against us. Behold, what an ignominious state you have placed us in! Not only thousands of my people are fallen, but thousands of yours as well—mostly of the chosen ones. And the land—the land itself—has it not suffered? All this mad treading on crops and burning of cattle! Now your own Caliph comes to you for succor, and what do you have to offer?" He passed among them, still darting fiery looks, adding, "Yet how could you, in the blindness of you hearts, foresee such a calamity? You were imprisoned in your own pettiness and hatred and jealousy!"

Slowly, he went back to his seat. As he was about to recline, the Wali implored, "Please Guirguis, this is no time for reproof. We are sorely pressed and must try to see how we can best meet the present situation."

Guirguis sat down—nay, he laid back and was wrapped in thought. For a few seconds, he was unaware of those around him. Then he came back, sat up, and said, "Well my lord, the only solution is to get the army ready and to send your messengers all over the land to recruit able men. What else do you need?"

A few voices exclaimed together, "What about the money needed?"

"Money needed?" retorted Guirguis sarcastically, "Put

the Patriarch back in prison."

"And Abba Moussa, too."

He gazed at them, then said very calmly, "This time it will not be for long, because you shall have to flee for your lives within a few short days."

Some paled at his words, others were infuriated. "You should be imprisoned as well. Better still, have that smooth tongue of yours cut."

Here, the Wali said fiercely, "I would rather have all your tongues cut."

Guirguis slowly added, "Whatever you may do to me or to my people, you cannot evade your doom."

At these words, one courtier completely lost his temper and shouted, "Do you hear, my lord, what he says?" Then, flinging his dagger at Guirguis, he said, "You accursed dog, take that from me!" But the dagger fell short of its aim.

Guirguis laughed outright, while murmurs of "charm" and "sorcery" were mumbled.

The Wali shouted, "What! Dare you behave thus in my presence? I tell you again, and all of you listen, I'd rather have all of your tongues cut than touch so much as a hair from Guirguis. By Allah! I'll have you punished and make you an example to the whole lot!"

He was about to clap his hands for his bodyguard to arrest the miscreant courtier, when Guirguis laid a restraining hand on him and said, "Nay, my lord, this is not the time for petty quarrels. Our land is threatened, and we cannot afford to stop and kill one man from among us."

The Wali stopped, looked at the misbehaving courtier—

who reddened and paled by turn—then said, "No one can deny the truth of your saying, for no one can evade his destiny."

Guirguis answered, "Whether he denies it or not will not make the slightest difference."

The Wali said, "Have it your way, I will forego his insolence for your sake only." With that, he dismissed his courtiers, keeping a few chosen ones to discuss the problem of defense, and assigned each his role. He then turned to Guirguis and said, "Please, convince that cousin of yours to be near at hand, for we shall surely need him."

Guirguis laughed, "You mean Doctor Mena?"

"Why, of course I do."

"I shall send for him, as he has left Al-Fustat sometime ago."

"I shall rely on you."

"Well, you know what it means when I give my word."

"I know it too well."

"Then allow me a twenty-four hours' leave and your fleetest Arab steed."

"I shall give you my white stallion, Al Bark, for a present; you know how fleet-footed he is. Only you be as prompt as your word."

Guirguis got up to leave. As the Wali shook hands with him, he said in subdued tones, "Oddly enough, you make me feel sorry for what has happened to your people."

Guirguis looked at him squarely and wistfully, then said very slowly, "That suffices me, my lord." Then raising his hand to his forehead, he saluted and departed.

Going out, he rushed to *Al-Muallakah* Church, where he lingered for a few short minutes. They were enough for him to pour forth all the anguish of his soul and the aspirations of his heart. Walking out, he repeated to himself, "At least before You, my God and my Heavenly Father, I can be myself: just a child of Yours, sorely tried, asking You to fill me with Your Grace that I may be able to carry on to the end, that I may go forth in Your service, strong in Your might." Then, committing himself to the protection of the saints—and above all, to the Blessed Virgin—he went home."

***

When Mena, like the Prodigal, had come to himself, he asked Abba Moussa about his parents and his brother's family. The holy man told him that he had deputed Pishoy to go with some trusty companions to carry the bodies off the battlefield and to have the church service chanted over them. With this mission fulfilled, Pishoy and his companions went to Samanoud.

Mena lifted up his eyes to meet the bishop's as he said, "I confess, I feel awed at times in face of Guirguis. Why, he was so impetuous a lad! What a man he now is! The Blessed Mother protect him, and may he live long and be accorded the joy of wedding Demiana!"

"Amen," rejoined Abba Moussa in deep solemnity, "She is a brave girl that sister of yours, and is certainly fit to be the wife of so valiant a man as Guirguis." With these words,

Mena took leave for Samanoud.

***

Mariam was so astonished to hear the footsteps of Guirguis at such an hour that she hastened to the door to meet him. He kissed her hand reverently and said without being asked, "Fear not, I am only being sent by the Wali to fetch cousin Mena, as his presence will doubtless be necessary these coming days. Pray for me that I succeed in my errands!"

Mariam laughed confidently, "Your cousin is obstinate and hot-headed, but he loves you very dearly, and I am sure he will not refuse you."

Half an hour later, Guirguis sped away in the midday sun for Samanoud.

For seven hours he sped along, sometimes slowing down a little to give the steed a respite. More than once, he got off and brought his horse a drink from some running stream. As he sped along, the thoughts whirled within his mind—happiness and woe, success and failure. As a refrain, the thought of Demiana came back and forth to him as a refreshing breeze softening the glare of the sun. She was still in Wissim; she could not leave it because Abba Moussa entrusted her with the responsibility of looking after all those living on the bishop's estate. In addition, all the bereaved within the vicinity flocked to the Mansion in quest of consolation. Stricken with grief, she remained at her post. The ever-vigilant Abba Moussa sent her a number of messages, in which he described to her in detail the fortitude and prowess of Guirguis. The consolation which these messages gave her was beyond measure. Early every morning, before going about her duty, she would slip into the church for a few minutes to gather the needed strength for the day.

On the eve of the day in which Guirguis let out his steam on the cowardly courtiers, she was sitting under the great sycamore in a dreamy mood. The whole scene passed before her eyes in every detail, until she finally saw him riding the white steed, rushing towards Samanoud. She was stirred to her depth. Rising up briskly, she entered the church and stood in silence before the sanctuary. Then acting on an inward impulse, she rushed up to her room and wrote a message to her beloved, which she dispatched the following morning.

Meanwhile, Guirguis sped on, the picture of Demiana spurring him onward. He wondered when he would be able to see her. "Soon enough," said the voice within him. He tried to still that voice in vain, for he well knew how true it was; it was a voice that never failed. Whose was it? Maybe Big Brother's... who knows? All he knew was that it was a trusted voice.

As he neared his uncle's house, his heart beat fast—faster than ever. For a few short seconds, he brought Al Bark to a standstill that he may give himself the chance to steady his aching heart. He had braved a danger and withstood many a foe without fear. But now, a little dread gripped him; the picture of the house with Youannis filled him with regret and sorrow. Nevertheless, he went steadily on. He heaved a sigh of relief when the silhouette of Mena appeared to him amid the flickering lights standing at the entrance of the house. He leaped off his horse, and with one stride was beside his cousin. The two men fell on each other's neck and wept silently for a few minutes.

Strangely enough, Mena was the first to speak, asking in surprise, "My dearest cousin, what brings you at this hour? Have you told Demiana of your coming?"

Guirguis opened his eyes in surprise, and said in a voice that shook with tumultuous emotion, "How could I? Is she here?"

In answer, Mena fumbled through his pockets and brought out Demiana's message, handing it to him and saying, "Lo, she is still in Wissim, the brave little girl. But about midday, her courier brought this letter."

Guirguis took the note, brought it to his lips in silence, then quietly said, "Let us go in to see my dear uncle and aunt, and to pay our due homage to Ageya and the boys."

Mena put his arm within his cousin's and said, "I told Abba Moussa that oftentimes I feel awed by you. At this moment, that same awe has seized me." Guirguis gave no reply; he seemed unaware of his cousin's remark. As they were going up the verandah steps, Mena asked, "Surely you have come here on a special mission. I know that you are not allowed out of the lion's den except for an urgent quest."

"Yes, cousin Mena. We will speak of that later. Now, let us center our attention on our beloved—those departed, and those here with us in the body."

The two men walked in, silent, but with their heads high. The parents of Youannis were sitting in the reception room, which was filled and emptied by the incessant flow of people coming in to express their sympathy. Thank God, they were alone for the moment. Guirguis hastened towards them, kissing their hands by turn, and was unable to utter a word. He pulled a low stool and sat facing them.

It was Youannis's mother who broke the silence. She laid a loving hand on his shoulder and said, "Guirguis, we each know how the other feels without any need for words. Your spirit must have been groaning within you while all along, you had to appear callous."

He laid his head on her knees and steadily said, "Yes, beloved aunt. Your heart tells you of all my grief, but it also tells you what Big Brother told me as his life was ebbing away: 'When one Torchbearer falls, the next in line must pick it up.'"

"You certainly have acted in complete obedience to these words, Guirguis, and in the midst of all our sorrow and grief, our hearts swell with pride at the mere thought of you."

He lifted up his head towards her and her husband, looking at each in turn, then murmured, "'We also are compassed about with so great a cloud of witnesses.' These are the words which my most beloved Abba Moussa invariably uses to greet me."

Youannis's father added, "Let us lay aside every weight and the sin which does so easily beset us, and let us run with patience the race that is set before us."

"Yes, Guirguis my son, we must shoulder our responsibility with dignity."

"Speaking of dignity, where is our dear Ageya?" queried Guirguis.

Mena hastily replied, "She is up with the two boys,

trying to answer their oftentimes unanswerable questions. When you see her, you will be inspired by her dignity and fortitude; she reminds herself daily that she is the wife of a hero who must bring up her two boys to also be valiant heroes."

Guirguis looked into the eyes of Mena and repeated in a whisper, "When one Torchbearer falls, the other must pick up the Torch..." and added "Will you lead me to where she is, that I may offer her my homage? Unfortunately, I must go back in haste."

Both parents asked in one voice, "Will you not spend the night with us? Even if only part of it."

"I gave my word to the Wali to be in Al-Fustat by noon."

"Then," said the mother, "I must order the preparation of the bath, that you may refresh yourself, then eat before setting off."

Guirguis looked at her, then at his uncle, then said, "Pray, allow Mena to come with me. I know he should be by your side, but then, the torchbearers must be ever on duty."

His uncle looked inquiringly, and Guirguis said, "The Caliph Marwan sent word that he is coming here in haste because he is being pursued by his enemies restlessly. He shall have to meet them in open battle on this dearly beloved land of ours. He may be here in a day or two. During such grave times, Mena will be urgently needed. The Wali has requested of me this service, that I come and fetch him."

Mena frowned, but faced his cousin squarely. He was about to open his mouth, when his father put his hand on his shoulders and said, "Mena, we were just now talking of the great cloud of witnesses... dare you make them feel ashamed because you refused to serve?"

"But—"

"There is no 'but' in the matter. Yes, they have treacherously dealt with us. Shall we turn traitors to all we hold dear because of that?"

Mena reddened. He bent over his father's hand and kissed it several times, then added, "I beg your pardon father." Then facing Guirguis once more, he said, "I shall prepare the horses and pack my medicines, while you bathe. And Good Mother of God, you have not even opened Demiana's note!"

His father said, "There Mena, what an example your cousin is. He offers his homage to us first, asks about Ageya and the boys, and delivers the Wali's message when all along, that note lies next to his heart."

"Well Guirguis, most valiant Torchbearer, come and greet Ageya. Then right away you will have the pleasure of reading Demiana's note." Mena put his arm in his cousin's, and they both walked out.

They went up to Ageya's room. Her mother-in-law had given her the news of their arrival when she had left to order the bath and the dinner, so her door was open, and both men walked in.

Guirguis took her hand in both of his, and for the space of a few seconds scanned her face with great affection. Then he kissed her hand and said, "Ageya, may our Heavenly Father fill your heart with His consolation, and envelop you and your boys with His tender mercies. You are indeed a wife worthy of a valiant man."

She answered in a voice that was barely above a whisper,

"May He overwhelm you with abounding grace, that you may be able to carry on." He then walked to the bedside of the two boys, who were already fast asleep, and knelt by them for a few seconds in silence.

Just then, an attendant knocked at the door to say that the bath was ready. Guirguis excused himself and followed him.

After the bath, he was left alone. It was only then that he brought out Demiana's note, reading it and kissing it by turn. Having read and reread it, he folded it lovingly and put it once again in the pocket next to his heart, then said, "My beloved Demiana, you are as brave as you are beautiful. You are indeed a wondrous gift from God to me."

Then rousing himself from his delectable reverie, he went downstairs to the dining room where they were all waiting for him. His look at Mena received the answer, "Yes, you grand taskmaster: the horses are ready, my medicines are packed, and I am taking with me two of my most promising disciples, for surely we will need more than one doctor."

"Well done, dearest cousin."

They ate and talked, and though their voices were subdued, yet their hearts were lightest since the fateful day. Guirguis told them of how Demiana foresaw his coming and sent her note of love and consolation and encouragement. After that, they all wanted to hear of what happened to him as he lived day in and day out in the very midst of the foes. He told them briefly what he went through, then added, "God's protection has so wonderfully overshadowed me, that they all believe I have invisible protectors—and indeed I do."

"Yes indeed," came the unanimous assent.

When dinner was over, Youannis's mother suggested that the travelers should have some sleep, but Guirguis said, "Believe me dearest aunt, the mere presence among you has enthused me with new strength, so with your permission, we will rest in the reception room to relax or doze, or chat, as the spirit wills." They all assented. When each had chosen his corner, Guirguis sat for some time at the feet of Youannis's mother and gave her Demiana's note, which she perused with tenderness. Returning it to him, she bent and kissed his forehead.

He, reclining on one of the divans, said, "It is so soothing to be among loved ones, whose love is a protection. It is such a contrast to my daily routine, where I have to be like a sentinel, and where jealousies and hatreds are corrosive." They all reclined, speaking at moments, dozing off at others, until they heard the church cantor next door church chanting the third watch of the midnight prayers.

At the first notes, Guirguis got up saying, "Mena my cousin, our time is up. We have about ten hours' ride before us because your horses are not as fleet as Al Bark. I think we should go first to the revered lady Mariam before presenting ourselves to the Wali, don't you agree?" Youannis's mother assented wholeheartedly, together with her husband and Ageya.

Guirguis tiptoed up to where the boys slept, knelt beside them in silence, then rushed downstairs. They walked into the church for a few minutes, then away sped Guirguis and his companions. The first hour they rode in silence, each wrapped in his own thoughts, then Guirguis began to relate some jokes to while away their journey.

No sooner did he finish than Mena said, "Guirguis, my dearly beloved, please tell us some of your adventures in the lion's den."

Guirguis instead preferred to describe to them how the two venerable prelates bore their imprisonment, and what crowds went to seek their blessing even when they were shut up in a cavernous hole. Thus, the journey back was full of consolation to them.

***

Twenty-four hours later to a minute, Guirguis, Mena, and his two assistants walked in to where the Wali and his courtiers assembled. Thereupon the Wali exclaimed, "As good as your word—even now. Come, sit by my side that I may entertain you for a change, for surely you are tired after your journey."

After introducing the two men, Guirguis sat down. The Wali then turned to Mena, saying, "Welcome Dr. Mena. Come, sit down on my other side to hear the tale I will relate to your cousin, for by Allah he is a magician, don't you agree?"

Mena laughed most heartily. "Yes my lord, truly he is. I told him that only last night." He sat down, and his two assistants sat next to him.

The Wali then told them that no sooner had Guirguis taken leave than Zoheir appeared, of all people. The mere mention of Zoheir's name made Mena sit up and bristle, contrary to Guirguis who relaxed back and even smiled. "Well, Zoheir sat an dabbled, then the conversation got heated and rose to such a pitch that suddenly Hussein—" here the Wali winked at Guirguis, who roared with laughter, while Mena looked puzzled at both. "Have patience Dr. Mena," The Wali explained, "Will you never learn from your cousin?"

"You just told me that he is a magician, where shall I learn magic?"

"Well," continued the Wali, "Hussein challenged Zoheir to a single combat, and all because of that magician next to me. Imagine that Hussein could not stand Zoheir's insolence against Guirguis, when only a few days ago he had aimed at him unsuccessfully with his dagger! I would have severely punished him had not Guirguis interceded for him." Then, reverting to his story, he continued, "The two men walked out, followed by a few others. Their absence lasted barely half and hour. Then men came back saying that Zoheir was killed and that Hussein was sorely wounded. Today I was told that he became unconscious. Maybe Mena can tell us what chance of life he has. Anyhow, when this incident happened, I said, 'surely Guirguis has some secret gift of Allah's, for those who have tried their best to hurt him have punished each other."

Mena ejaculated impetuously, "'Vengeance is mine, I will repay,' saith the Lord."[65] Then toning down, he added, "And that, in the absence of Guirguis, too."

During these short moments, Guirguis was lost in thought and seemed again remote from all those around him. The vision of Demiana dragged into the midst of this very hall by her own cousin out of sheer spite filled his

---

65 Deut. 32:35.

mind, only to be succeeded by that other picture of Zoheir's perfidy a few days ago. All his pettiness and bursts of jealousy he had displayed came in between. Guirguis remembered also that he needed all the forces of his higher self to control the fury that raged within his soul whenever he saw Zoheir or thought of him. Now he felt sorry for him, for surely he could have been a better man if he had people who could guide him along the upright path.

Slowly, Guirguis sat up. Then, he said very soberly, "I am sorry for the two of them. In all honesty, I am."

The Wali sighed, "You baffle me, as you always do. Pray, why waste your sympathy on two rascals?"

"Rascals indeed, but I am sorry all the same, and I beg my dear cousin Mena to see Hussein right away, as he might be of service to him."

Mena blinked a little, then said somewhat brokenly, "Well, just to please you, I will see him. But indeed, you are a man of priceless worth." Then he got up, taking leave of the Wali, and beckoned his two assistants to go to the wounded man.

They had barely reached the door of the hall when a messenger came to say that Hussein had already breathed his last.

The Wali shook his head, "Your services are not needed any longer, Dr. Mena. He could not evade his doom, as your cousin told him two days ago." Then, turning to Guirguis, he said, "As for you, dear friend, to show you how much I appreciate your service, I shall give you another twenty-four hours leave for your own leisure. I have always wanted you near me, but you well deserve a breathing space. Only request that Dr. Mena to keep by my side in your absence."

Mena flushed and said, "You know fully well, my lord, that I can never replace my cousin. His wit..."

Guirguis stood up, then smiling naughtily at Mena, he said, "I give you my word for him. He may be a poor substitute, but he'll do all the same." Turning to Mena he said, "You will stay by the side of my lord, won't you?" Mena acquiesced by a nod. "That's a promise!"

"Yes indeed. Can I disobey you?"

"And keep your assistants within beck and call."

The three men answered in unison, "At your bidding."

The Wali turned to Guirguis and said, "My friend, I hope Al Bark has served you well."

"Indeed my lord, he well deserves his name.[66] Thank you for giving him to me, and more than thank you for this consideratenes towards me." Raising his hand to his forehead, he saluted and walked out. As usual, he went first to *Al-Muallakah* Church in gratitude to the Heavenly Father, then rode home.

Mariam rushed to the door at the sound of his footsteps and smiled contentedly as she saw him radiant.

He kissed each of her hands by turn, then said, "Imagine that I have another twenty-four hours in which to breathe freely!"

Mariam, still smiling, said, "Holy Mother of God, your mood and your voice today are the same as when you discovered you were in love with Demiana."

---

66 *Bark* means "lightning" in Arabic.

"Yes, my most angelic cousin. I have not felt as serene or as light-hearted for a long time."

"I shall prepare your bag for you. In the meantime, please eat something before you leave."

In half an hour, Guirguis was bounding downstairs. It was almost three o'clock when he jumped on the back of Al Bark saying, "My newly-acquired friend, we shall make a shorter journey this time, and one very near to my heart." Al Bark bounded off sensing his master's mood.

"Well, dear heart," mused Guirguis, "'Soon enough' is even sooner than I could have surmised, for here I am on my way to Demiana within twenty-four hours of my declaration!" The picture of Wissim filled his horizon at that moment, for had it not been his haven since the first great upheaval of his life? And had he not found such a haven with a most understanding and kindly guide as Abba Moussa? What would have become of him? "But for the grace of God," he murmured unto himself, and his thoughts flitted off to the time when he first met Demiana, while fond memory brought to light other days around him.

Suddenly, he pulled himself by force of will; he had to guide his horse. This was not his dear old Meshir who could gallop blind-folded to Wissim, this was a stranger that had to be introduced to the journey, then to the people at the beloved sanctuary. So he deftly directed the horse and warmed it up to its full speed.

Within an hour, he slowed into the garden of the Mansion. It did not surprise him to find Demiana on the lookout near the gate. He jumped off his horse and rushed towards her as she rushed towards him. He enfolded her within his arms while she rested her head against his breast for a few seconds. Then she lifted her eyes to him and he kissed her again and again. Neither seemed to find any words to say.

Suddenly, Guirguis saw Abba Moussa on the verandah, so he carried Demiana and ran towards him asking, "How did you come here, holy father?"

The holy man beamed at Guirguis as he put Demiana on her feet and bent to kiss his hand. Then he said, "I came early this morning to catch you playing truant."

The three laughed, and Demiana said, "Do you sometimes play truant, Guirguis?"

Abba Moussa said, "Nay, not so my daughter. He Who counts our hair has so softened the heart of the Wali, that he gave his favorite a leave of twenty-four hours."

Guirguis radiantly said, "I know that you're clairvoyant, and I am certainly flattered that you came to welcome me in this beloved spot."

Abba Moussa placed himself between the two lovers, surrounded each of them with an arm, and said, "Come my beloved to the church, that we may offer our thanks. Then I shall leave you until dinner time."

After prayer, the saintly man left them. The two sat under the big sycamore, talking at moments, keeping silent in others. They were content to be together in this peaceful corner after all the terrible upheavals, the bereavements, the worry, and the agony.

They were oblivious of time until they heard Pishoi's familiar footsteps. In his deep bass voice, he said in the semi-darkness, "Dear friends, our holy father is waiting for you." They got up immediately and went in. The dining room was full of people who rushed to see their beloved bishop—and Guirguis, who had become almost a legend to them. As soon as he entered, shouts of endearment and welcome met him.

He was about to shake hands with each, when Abba Moussa took hold of his hand and led him and Demiana to the chairs on either side of his. He said, "Dear children, one and all, this young man has been traveling and has not eaten one morsel since his arrival earlier this afternoon, so please excuse him." With these words, he lifted up his arms to say grace, after which they all sat down and began their meal. A sense of well-being pervaded them all.

When dinner was over, they sat in the reception room while more people flocked in. Guirguis was showered with questions. He had to tell them of Zoheir's treason. Finding that Demiana turned crimson at the mere mention of his name, he added, "Calm down my dearest, for he has already gone to give account of his stewardship."

"You mean he is already dead?"

"Yes."

"But surely not in the battle?"

"No, in single combat. Have patience, and I will tell you the whole of it in detail."

"I shall keep very silent."

All eyes were fixed on him, while his were fixed on Abba Moussa and Demiana by turn as he related to them the incidents of the last few days, beginning with the arrival of the Caliph's messenger.

When he reached the end of his account, Abba Moussa said, "You are a consummate artist, my son. You whiled away our time with such ease, that in all fairness, you must go and sleep directly. You barely have time to rest before you resume your journey. No wonder the Wali cannot part with you! So goodnight, and may the blessings of all the saints and of the Blessed Mother of God be with you." With that Guirguis went up to sleep, asking Pishoi to wake him up at dawn.

***

When Guirguis came down the following day, the whole town seemed to have collected in the garden of the Mansion. No sooner did they see him than they cheered him and sent up their prayers for him. Abba Moussa was in church already; Guirguis and Demiana walked towards it, followed by the people. When the prayers ended, Abba Moussa came out, leaning with one arm on Guirguis and the other on Demiana. Pishoi stood by the gate, holding Al Bark. As the young hero jumped on its back, the holy man said, "Only a few more days, my son. It is true they will be full of trials and tribulations, but they will be short. Tomorrow evening, by God's grace, I shall be at Babylon. Godspeed, and may the blessings of the saints sustain you unto the end."

Guirguis spurred his steed, and as it galloped away, cheers rent the morning sky; everyone was loudly invoking the saints to protect and strengthen him.

He went home to tell Mariam of the joy which filled his heart and of the words of Abba Moussa. As usual, she was waiting for him at the top of the stairs, and he kissed her hands.

She said, "Guirguis, my son, though you still have two more hours of freedom, still you must forego them. A messenger has just passed asking about you, saying that the Wali needs you."

"Well, I have been in Paradise dearest cousin. So I can afford to forego the two hours. How infinitely kind our Heavenly Father is! But tell me, has Mena come home?"

"No, he spent the night at the Wali's house—him and his two assistants."

"Did the messenger leave any message?"

"No, he simply said that the Wali wants you."

"Well, off I go."

He ran lightly downstairs, and once more mounted Al Bark. A few minutes later, he walked into the Wali's presence.

"Welcome, welcome my good friend. I am glad to see you."

Guirguis smiled at Mena as he got up to cede his place, so he asked, "Say, my lord, how did this cousin of mine behave?"

"Truly, he was a fine companion."

Mena hastily cut in: "Not half as fine as you, cousin of mine."

The Wali then told Guirguis that they were to leave for the Red Sea towards Belbeis, as news came that Marwan would be arriving shortly. "And," the Wali added, "I want you to come along with me, you sorcerer."

Guirguis laughed so heartily that the Wali said, "I fear that you have added to your store of magic during your leave. Allah alone knows what spirit you were consulting."

Guirguis laughed again saying, "Truly, my lord, I was lucky to meet more than one angel last night. But say, when are we to leave?"

"In an hour's time,"

"What about Mena and his assistants?"

"No need for them yet."

"Then allow me to return home, and I shall meet you within an hour in front of your gate."

"Agreed."

***

Guirguis barely reached home, and had only saluted Mariam, when one of his attendants came in to say that the gatekeeper has sent a messenger: a hooded horseman was asking to see him in great urgency. Guirguis jumped up from his seat, but Mariam caught him by the sleeve.

Their eyes spoke volumes in a few fleeting seconds, then Guirguis said, "Mariam, dearest cousin, you know I have learned by experience to listen to that voice within."

She nodded still fixing him with her gaze, as he continued, "Well, this honest guide is telling me that it is a friend—and not a foe—who is by the gate; so by your leave..." She shook her head in assent and let go of his sleeve. He bent and kissed her hands, then walked out.

A few minutes later, she heard him coming up the stairs laughing and saying, "Welcome to my home, my lord. We have been friends for so long, but you have yet to honor me with a visit." Both men walked in to find Mariam sitting on the divan where Guirguis had left her. He bowed to her, then turning to his guest, Guirguis said, "My lord, this is Lady Mariam, wife of Big—er, sorry—of my big brother, who was both brother and father to me."

The Wali shook hands with her, then said, "Today I come to you as a friend, not as the Wali. That is why I came to your house, that in its privacy I may freely open my heart without fear of betrayal."

Mariam and Guirguis exchanged fleeting glances. She then got up, but the Wali said, "Pray, lady, don't go."

She answered, "I shall be with you in a minute." Indeed, she returned shortly with an attendant who was carrying a tray of fruits and some soothing drinks.

While they ate and drank, the Wali said, "Of late, you have taught me many lessons, Guirguis, and I have grown very fond of you. I wanted you to come with me when I go to meet the Caliph. But no sooner did I part with you than a messenger arrived to report that Marwan is in a mad mood, seized with the lust for destruction."

Guirguis cut in, "But, my lord—"

"No, my friend. I know your integrity and your willingness to sacrifice your very life. But you are a young man, and there is a beautiful young lady eagerly awaiting your safety. I would hate to squander your life." He was silent, and so were his hosts. Then, turning to Mariam, he said, "Can you believe that I, who once desired to kill

Guirguis, and who flogged him publicly and threw him into prison, would be thus conquered by him?"

She answered impulsively, "That is God's grace."

The Wali nodded in assent, then standing up, said, "I shall have to be going. Because I do not know whether fortune or misfortune will be our lot, I will bid you adieu. May Allah protect you." For the first time, the Wali fell on the neck of Guirguis and kissed him. Then hooding himself, he bowed towards Mariam and walked out, with Guirguis escorting him to the gate of the Coptic Quarter.

Rushing back, he found Mariam kneeling before the icon of the Blessed Virgin in silent gratitude, and he knelt down beside her. A few minutes later, he exclaimed, "How manifold are Thy mercies, O Heavenly Father!" After another moment of silence, he rose up saying, "And now to work, cousin dearest. I must dispatch as many couriers to as many of our people as possible to forewarn them of the impending catastrophe." Then calling on his clerk, he dictated to him the message he desired to convey and ordered him to see that it reached the biggest number of people.

***

A little before sunset, Guirguis went to *Al-Muallakah* Church in quest of Abba Moussa. He reached its doorway at the very moment this venerable bishop was dismounting his palanquin.

"Welcome, welcome holy father," and he kissed his hands with added zeal.

The man of God beamed, remarking, "Today, you are as the little boy I knew! Why, you radiate with joy! Come, tell me all about it."

They went into the church. Guirguis gave a detailed account of the Wali's behavior, after which Abba Moussa and all those with him declared, "Glory to God."

After chanting the Vespers, the venerable bishop went home with Guirguis. There, they planned how best they could help their people to evade the on-rushing catastrophe.

As they were conferring together, Guirguis suddenly remarked, "Excuse me, holy father, we seem to have forgotten we should send word to our honored Patriarch."

"Dear son, our venerated Patriarch was arrested this very morning by the Turkish general sent by Marwan. And I warn you that I will be arrested, too. But grieve not; it will only be for a few days."

***

The few days foretold by the bishop were indeed a few in number, but they seemed endless in the amount of destruction and horror committed therein. Al-Fustat was burned by order of Marwan, but the priests and layman served vigilant shifts to save the churches and the adjoining houses from the conflagration.

Before beginning the battle, Marwan ordered the arrest of Abba Moussa, together with several monks and clergymen. The battle itself was fierce indeed; Marwan, pursued by his enemies, had to flee southward. Within ten days, he and one of his sons were killed, and his army was annihilated. The enemy won an overwhelming victory.

When the trumpet heralded the cessation of fighting, Guirguis went out with Mena in search of the Wali. After a few hours, they found him sorely wounded but aware enough to recognize them. Mena tried his skill, but it was fruitless; the one-time enemy who had become a friend died with his head resting on the lap of Guirguis.

***

A week after the declaration of peace, the crowds flocked to Wissim. Guirguis and Demiana were to be united in holy wedlock by their beloved Abba Moussa. The ceremony was grand indeed, but the celebrations were sobered down by the late bereavements. Their hearts, though joyous, were broken. But they exulted in the confidence that their heavenly Father is mindful of even a cup of cold water given in His name.

Appendix A

On this day of the year 483 A.M. (March 12th, 767 A.D.), the holy father Anba Khail (Mikhail), the forty-sixth Pope of the See of St. Mark, departed. This father was a monk in the monastery of St. Macarius, and he was knowledgeable and ascetic. When Pope Theodorus, the forty-fifth Patriarch, his predecessor, departed, the bishops of Lower Egypt (Delta) and the priests of Alexandria gathered in the church of Anba Shenouda in Cairo.

A Dispute arose among them about who was fit [for the Papal Throne], and finally they called Anba Moussa, Bishop of Ouseem (Wissim), and Anba Petros, Bishop of Mariout. When they arrived, Anba Moussa found the priests of Alexandria obstinate, and he rebuked them for that, dismissing them that night so their minds and souls might calm down. When they met the next day, he mentioned to them the name of the priest Khail the monk in the monastery of St. Macarius. They unanimously agreed to his choice and obtained a decree from the Governor of Egypt to the elders of the wilderness of Sheheet (Wadi El-Natroun) to bring him from the monastery. On their way, when they arrived to Giza, they found Father Khail coming along with some elders to fulfill a certain task connected with the monastery. They seized him, bound him, and took him to Alexandria where they ordained him Patriarch on the 17th of Tute, year 460 A.M. (September 14th., year 743

---

67 The Synexarion is a compilation of daily hagiographies.

A.D.). There had been a drought in the city of Alexandria for two years, and on that day the rain fell heavily for three days, and the people of Alexandria considered that a good omen.

During the papacy of this father was the reign of Marawan, the last of the Khalifas of the Umayyad rule, and governor Hefs Ebn El-Walid. Many great tribulations fell upon the believers [during that time].

A large number of the believers fled from Egypt, and the number of those who denied Christ was twenty-four thousand. Because of that, the Patriarch was in great sorrow until God perished those were responsible. This father endured many difficulties from Abdel Malek Ebn-Marawan, the new governor. He imprisoned, beaten, chained, and tortured him with many other ways of painful tortures, then he released him. The Patriarch went to Upper Egypt to collect alms and when he came back, the Governor took the money from him and threw him back in prison. When Keriakos, king of Nuba, knew that, he was extremely enraged. He prepared one hundred thousand soldiers and marched down to Egypt. Going through, Upper Egypt he slew all the Muslims that he met, until he reached Al-Fustat (Cairo). He camped around the city threatening to destroy it. When Abdel Malek the Governor saw the army surrounding the city and that all this had taken place for the sake of the Patriarch, he became terrified, so he released him from prison with great honor. The Governor entreated the Patriarch to mediate peace between him and the king of Nuba. The Patriarch agreed to his request, so he went with some of the clergy to meet the king and asked him to accept peace from Abdel Malek, which the king accepted and returned back. Abdel Malek respected the Christians and lifted up all his retribution. When the father the Patriarch prayed for the sake of the Governor's daughter, who was possessed with an unclean spirit, the unclean spirit left her, and the Governor increased his respect for the Christians.

This father debated with Cosmas the Melchite Patriarch concerning the Hypostatic Union. Pope Khail wrote him a letter, signed it along with his bishops, which said in it: "It is not right to say that Christ has two distinct Natures or two distinct Persons after the Hypostatic Union." Cosmas was convinced with that and asked to become a bishop under the authority of Anba Khail.

When Anba Khail completed his strife, he departed to the Lord whom he loved after he had spent on the Chair of St. Mark twenty-three and half years.

May his prayers be with us and Glory be to God forever. Amen.

Appendix B

PORTRAIT OF A HISTORIAN
IRIS HABIB EL-MASRI (1910-1994) AUTHOR
OF THE STORY OF THE COPTIC CHURCH

COMPILED AND WRITTEN BY
DORA HABIB EL-MASRI.

From her early youth, the dynamic power of the Coptic Church attracted her, and she started studying earnestly and with reverence everything that pertained to it: the language, the Liturgy, the rituals, the prayers and the hymns. She loved it whole-heartedly and decided to dedicate her life in pursuit of studying its history. She chose to be a nun, not in a convent, but in the world at large. She felt that she had a mission to fulfill. There was an inward voice calling her and an invisible hand guiding her. Her mind was tuned to the frequency of God's divine love and to the Grace of Jesus Christ. The messages fully reached her heart and were the power that kept her working faithfully all her life. Her eyes were set on the goal she wanted to achieve, and that was to write the history of the magnificent Coptic Church, to make it known to the world.

Iris had fortitude of character, the power of perseverance, and the sincere efforts to gain a vast knowledge about her beloved Coptic Church. She spent all her life in research so as to write the true story of Christianity in Egypt. She held the pen in her hand and started writing and she never, ever put it down or looked backwards, but went steadily forwards, with an indomitable spirit, to write that great history. Iris was adamant in her zeal and perseverance. She had a good command of the language and expressed herself in clear, lucid words that were a joy to the reader. All these qualities combined together made her history books a pure source of knowledge.

Iris Habib El-Masri is the only woman historian in Egypt. She is also the only person who wrote the complete history of the Church which started with the advent of St. Mark to Alexandria in the year sixty-one AD, until the year nineteen hundred seventy one, the time of Pope Kyrillos VI, the 116th pope on the See of Alexandria. She wrote nineteen hundred years of history in nine volumes, entitled *The Story of the Coptic Church*.

In the memoirs of Iris, I found the following note about her experience in reading the Holy Bible:

> I am holding steadfastly to the true Coptic Orthodox faith, which is based firmly on the continuity of both the Old and the New Testaments. I have been brought up and nourished by reading all the books of the Holy Bible. I read them gradually, consecutively, and continuously and thought deeply of their contents. In the many books which I have written and which God Almighty has given me the power to accomplish, I have relied faithfully on verses from the Bible. To me, the Holy Bible beginning with the book of Genesis and ending with the book of Revelation was the pure source from which I drank and the highest reference for me in my books. Every time I read it, the teachings I found in it became clearer. The Holy

Spirit with its perpetual intercession aided me and with its power illuminated my mind. This enhanced my understanding of the meaning of the words which I read and I always discovered new things for my spiritual needs.

Iris read the Holy Bible with the eyes of her mind. She fully understood the Grace and Truth of the new life which Jesus Christ bestowed freely on those who believed in Him. Jesus Christ often reprimanded His listeners and wanted them to understand His words. He admonished those who have ears but do not hear and have eyes but do not see. Jesus did not ration the gifts of the Spirit but granted them bountifully to all those who accepted them with faith. When Jesus spoke to the two disciples of Emmaus, He was surprised to find them slow of heart to believe all that the prophets spoke about Him. He interpreted to them what referred to Him in all the Scriptures of the Old Testament, then their eyes were opened. Later St. Paul writes in the Epistle to the Romans: "Be ye transformed by the renewal of your minds, for you have not received the spirit of bondage again to fear, but you received the spirit of adoption whereby we say Abba, Father.[68]"

Iris was renewed in the spirit of her mind and she put on the new self. Her heart was enlightened and she followed Jesus Christ in the regeneration. She continuously gave thanks for this new life. She expressed her thanks truthfully and honestly in every book she wrote, whether it was a history book or otherwise. For example, in the foreword of her sixth volume she wrote,

---

68 Rom. 8:15.

I give thanks with humility and gratitude to the bountiful gifts with which God Almighty has overflowed on me. However many thanks I give, they will never be enough. How can I, the weak limited creature, give enough thanks to the Unlimited Creator?

In this same volume, she introduces her book as follows:

To all those who love the Church which we have inherited from our ancestors. To all those who care that our Coptic Church remains with its own integrity, I introduce to them this volume of *The Story of the Coptic Church,* praying to God, Father of the Church, to enlighten our vision so that we will go on, steadily and gratefully, to hand over our valuable treasure whole and beautiful to our children just as we have received it from our ancestors.

The first four volumes of *The Story of the Coptic Church* were supervised by the saintly Rev. Fr. Bishoy Kamel, Pastor of the Church of St. George in Sporting, Alexandria. He always encouraged her to complete her task and to write this story to the end. It was Father Bishoy who sent the drafts of these volumes, one by one to the printer and it was he who received them to be sold and distributed by the Church of St. George, to the benefit of the Church, as it was the wish of Iris.

Clergy and laymen alike esteemed her as a person and praised her as a historian. Three consecutive Popes of the See of Alexandria gave her important assignments: Pope

Youssab II assigned her in 1954 to be his private secretary for the correspondence with The World Council of Churches.

Pope Kyrillos VI appointed her in 1966 as Counsellor to Coptic Girls. The following is his letter of appointment:

October 20, 1966.

Baba 10,1683

The Blessed Daughter Iris Habib El Masri,

Blessings be upon you and on your behalf devout invocations. Being cognizant of your consuming zeal, your mature judgement, your loyalty and devotion to the Church and its members, of your unflagging concern for the welfare and the flourishing moral, social and cultural future of the young girls of the Coptic Orthodox faith, and of your dedication to the inculcating of the ORTHODOX TEACHINGS AND TRADITIONS of the Church in these young girls so that they may become worthy examples and virtuous models to all others in our beloved country, and all will see their good deeds and glorify God thereby. We have seen fit to decree your appointment as Counsellor to Coptic Girls, holding meetings with them in the assembly halls adjoining the two churches of the great saints Mark the Evangelist and George the Martyr in Heliopolis as well as those other adjoining coptic churches. You are to be responsible for fixing the time and place of the meetings and for giving regular weekly lectures, notices of which are to be inserted in the newspapers, instructing the girls spiritually, morally and socially that they may grow more attached and more loyal to the Coptic Church and to their beloved motherland. We have no doubt that you will prove yourself worthy of the great task with which we have charged you, certain that you will inform us periodically of your diverse activities and will thus assure us of your whole-hearted strivings in this blessed field. May God Almighty help, guide and bless your endeavors for the good of the Church and its blessed girls.

May His Grace overshadow you and His Arm protect you. To Him be praise and thanksgiving forever.

Pope Kyrillos VI

Patriarch of the Coptic Church

In 1972 Pope Shenouda III appointed Iris a member on the committee to rewrite the new synaxarium. Also in the same year, His Holiness wrote to her the following testimony:

Coptic Orthodox Patriarchate Papal Residence

The Coptic Orthodox Patriarchate testifies that Miss Iris Habib El-Masri is a deaconess in the Coptic Church serving in the ecclesiastical field for thirty years. She has served with all diligence and efficiency in child education and in delivering religious lectures to university students, both young men and young women. She has also taught Church history in the Higher Institute of Coptic Studies. Her books on the Coptic Church are valuable and comprehensive. She deserves to be congratulated and appreciated for them and we wish them a wide circulation.

Miss Iris is from a well-known Coptic family closely linked to the Church and sharing in its diverse activities.

Signed Pope Shenouda of Alexandria and the
See of Saint Mark, Sealed with the Papal Seal.

Dated 6/25/1972

In 1974 Iris went to London with her brother Sami El-Masri who was appointed director of the Egyptian State Bureau for Tourism in London. She wanted to have access to the famous Library of the British Museum and other university libraries. H.G. Bishop Gregorios, bishop of Higher Theological Studies and Coptic Culture and Scientific Research, who was at that time the Rector of the Institute of Coptic Studies at Anba Rweiss, wrote for Iris the following certificate:

To Whom It May Concern:

This is to certify that Professor Iris Habib El-Masri has been since 1954 professor of Coptic Church History in our Institute of Coptic Studies. Professor Iris is the author of The Story of the Church [of Egypt] and she is authoritative on the subject. She is highly estimated for her erudition and vast knowledge in history. She is of good Christian character and high sense of duty.

I recommend Miss Iris El-Masri as a good representative of our Coptic Orthodox Church.

Signed and sealed.

Dated September 26, 1974.

H.G. Bishop Moussa, Bishop of Youth, in a recorded interview with Iris in 1987, started by saying: "Today we are guests of our able Professor Iris. Many people have read with admiration her magnificent historical volumes written about the Coptic Church, beginning from the first century until our present time. We are happy that we have seen her and that we have heard her." After this introduction, His Grace asked Iris to relate to him how she started her great love for the Coptic Church. Iris then spoke with fervor and delight about her great love of the Coptic Church.

Now I will record the words of the venerable Father Matta El Meskeen (Matthew the Poor), the great scholar and theologian. In the introduction of Iris's fifth volume of *The Story of the Coptic Church*, he writes:

I reviewed your book word by word, and in all truth, I found it written with zeal and accuracy, combined with the sense of nationalism and deep loyalty to your faith. This book is considered a living part of our Egyptian heritage, the like of which we rarely find. It has great influence on the national spirit. I thank God that the series of your valuable history books are written with such a magnificent portrayal of our history which is a long story written with blood and tears. But our history remained vibrant and strong all through the centuries. It is a story that awakens the mind to the great glories of our spiritual and national existence.

Again in the introduction to the eighth volume, Father Matta El Meskeen writes:

In this volume we have a vision of the author herself. We see in her the qualities of the persevering historian who is always searching the books. This volume is a great addition to her unique historical books. It relates the story of Church and Country in their struggle against foreign occupation. Iris records in this volume the lives of some contemporaries: saints, laymen, scientists and artists, and also some ordinary people who live in obscurity but have a high spiritual life. History is life and their lives were mentioned as part of the Church. In this volume the author was elevated above this world to get inspired from the highest heavens.

Now I will mention the loving and sincere words of the Reverend Father Mikhail Saad, Pastor of the Church of St. Mary and St. Joseph in Smouha, Alexandria. He was a gifted preacher with the ability of the teacher who could explain vividly and ardently the words of the Holy Bible to the congregation. He had power and tenacity through his trust in the Grace of our Lord Jesus Christ and was able to build the grand house of grace in the vicinity of the Church. Fr. Mikhail Saad wrote more than once about Iris. I chose from the article which he wrote on the occasion of the fortieth day of her departure from this world. He wrote a tender message of loyalty to the memory of Iris. He invoked blessings and peace to her soul in the eternal abode in the Kingdom of Heaven. Then he describes her great achievements of knowledge that made known to the world the treasures of our fathers. He quotes the words of our Lord when He said, "Every scribe who has been instructed in the Kingdom of Heaven is like the head of a household who brings from his store room both the new and the old" (Matt. 13:52). Then he describes Iris as the person who renounced the vanity of this world and lived the life of a wise virgin whose lamp glittered with holy oil and who was always ready to meet the bridegroom. She held fast to faith, hope, and charity and always strove eagerly for the greatest of gifts which is love that remains forever.

It is not only the clergy who esteemed Iris, but also laymen praised her and valued her historical books. In the second volume Iris wrote about the entry of the Arabs into Egypt. She sent a copy to Professor Mohamed Mahmoud El-Sayad, who was at that time the Vice President of Ein Shams University. After reading her book, he sent her a letter on the top of which was written:

In Recognition of Goodwill. To the respected professor Iris Habib El-Masri,

Best salutations. I received with thanks your valuable book The Story of the Coptic Church. I read it and found that it contained the accuracy of the historian who knows the details of the subject about which he is writing. I hope that God will guide you to complete this unique story in your clear and excellent style. This is a big service to our country because the Coptic Church is a part of our national history which is dear to all of us. Egypt is proud that it was always a defender of religions. The people lived together along the centuries as brethren. They loved God and Country. All religions call for virtue and goodness. Egypt never deviated from sanctifying these qualities.

I congratulate you for your great efforts and thank you for presenting to me your book.

With my best wishes.

Signed and dated March 1, 1968

Iris also received a letter from Dr.Hassan Ragab, director of the Institute of Papyrus Research:

To the respected historian Iris Habib El-Masri,

Best salutations. I received with thanks your encyclopedic books about "The Story of the Coptic Church," which you have graciously donated to the library of my institute. I read and admired them for many reasons, foremost of which the orderly and accurate way in writing their contents and the information about the history of Christianity in Egypt. This history is a part of our national heritage which all Egyptians endear with pride. Secondly, I register my admiration for your indomitable spirit of research with such great strength and continuous perseverance. You read many references in different languages in order to give the true and vast knowledge to the reader. You spent many years of your life to achieve this goal. I ask God Almighty to prolong your life for the noble efforts you are doing which are for the service of both religion and country.

Your books have filled a big gap in the library of my institute. May God grant you His blessings.

Signed and dated October 1, 1984.

Iris received hundreds of letters from many thinkers and writers, from educated people and from simple people. They all expressed, everyone in his own style, the love and admiration for her.

Scholarship in Philadelphia

Iris was granted a scholarship by the International Federation of University Women to make research studies for one year in the United States. She asked of the committee of the Federation to choose for her a university that has the best professor in Coptology. Professor Cyrus Gordon was widely known at that time in 1952-1953 as the best Coptologist in the United States. He was at Dropsie College in Philadelphia. She studied under his tutorship and had access to many manuscripts. There was a Coptic manuscript which was bought by an American who donated it to the university and no one had read it before. Dr. Gordon told Iris that he was waiting for a Copt to come and unfold it and study its contents.

After her return from the United States, she received a letter from Dr. Gordon in which he wrote: "You were lucky to be born a Copt, but it is exclusively to your credit that you have built so creatively on your heritage. To inherit is not enough, we also have to build on our inheritance constructively."

Iris also received a letter from the president of Dropsie College in which he wrote,

> I am happy that we were able to afford the opportunities of study and research to you, and we are gratified that you made such excellent progress under the guidance of Professor Gordon. You were not only an outstanding student at the College, but you also made a very deep impression upon the larger community in Philadelphia by interpreting your country and its aspirations to important segments of the American population.
>
> *Signed Abraham Neuman*
> *Dated June 12 1953.*

During her stay in the United States that year, Iris gave 58 lectures about the Coptic Church and about Egypt from the broadcasting and television stations, in the Women's International League, and in the branches of the Federation of University Women.

Iris's first English edition of *The Story of the Coptic Church* was published in 1975 by the Middle East Council of Churches. When this edition became out of print, a second edition was published in 1982 by the Monastery of Abba Bishoi in California. Father Pachom Abba Bishoi, priest and monk, wrote in the introduction: "The author voluntarily did more than her best to fulfill this great work. We consider sister Iris El-Masri the only historian in the

Coptic Church at the present time."

The second edition also became out of print and a third edition was published in 1987. It was published by St. Fam Coptic Association in California and supervised by H. G. Bishop Antonios Markos, bishop of African Affairs. In the preface he wrote:

> Your heart will be touched by this faithful report of the Coptic Church. The author has spent years in research of ancient records in libraries of many nations to give us the book you now hold in your hand. It is in two volumes. Due to the high demand of The Story of the Coptic Church by individual Christians, Christian Institutions, libraries and the interested elite all over the world, the first two editions of such a book in the English language were sold out. There is a great need for the third edition in English language, which presents the true story of the Church of Christ in Egypt which has persisted for almost 2000 years. We feel it must be told to the world.
>
> Everybody who reads such a book has been touched by the faithful Christians of Egypt, God's Children, who have suffered for Christ and remained true through centuries.We trust your heart will be greatly blessed as you read this amazing book.
>
> *Signed Bishop Antonios Markos*

In the Epilogue of the English book, The Story of the Coptic Church, Iris writes:

The present-day Father of the Coptic Church is Abba Shenouda III, the 117th Pope in the glorious succession of St.Mark. The Church is more alive and revitalized than ever. A veritable new reawakening is evidenced by the amazing growth in the number of new churches continuously being built and always full to overflowing by the number of university educated young men and women who have entered the priesthood, the monasteries and the convents, and by the immense growth of Sunday Schools. What is more vital is the immense growth of awareness among Copts to the wonders of their Church. Apart from expanding and developing within its own boundaries, the Coptic Church has extended in a surprising way far beyond those boundaries. It is now a member of the World Council of Churches, The Middle East Council of Churches, and the All African Council of Churches. At the same time, churches have been founded in the U.S.A and Canada, and also in England, Italy, France, Germany, Australia and Africa.

So, although the story of the Copts as recorded in this book will end here, the story of the Copts as a living active people and of their Mother Church that has played the main role in keeping them active and living is still a continuous story. It is both heartening and full of promise, and it reinforces the confidence held by their majority, that through the Grace of God they will continue to have a story worth telling until time is swallowed up into eternity.

I have delineated highlights of the life of the great historian Iris Habib El- Masri. I would like to add that Iris lived humbly and lovingly. She was an ascetic. She fasted all the fasts and she daily recited the prayers of the Agpeya which she knew by heart. Her room was like a shrine; the walls were decorated with pictures of saints, and there was always a light in front of the picture of Saint Mary. The moment one entered that room, one felt a peaceful atmosphere. In that peaceful atmosphere, Iris worked through the quiet hours of the night until the early hours of dawn.